MW01264827

Page Zaplendam
believes in keeping tne wonder in life. She pursues
writing paranormal and dystopian fiction while juggling
home, crafts, and a large family. Fans can keep up with
her writing exploits at pagezaplendam.com or on her
facebook page.

Order of the Blood

The Unofficial Chronicles
Of John Grissom

Page Zaplendam

Order of the Blood: The Unofficial Chronicles of John Grissom

This is a work of fiction. Any similarity between the characters and situations within its pages and places or persons, living or dead, is unintentional and co-incidental.

Cover Photography from dreamstime.com
Cover Art by Page Zaplendam and C.E.

Contents

CHAPTER 1

LONDON 1809

He only noticed her because she arrived late. Of course, as would be apparent to everyone there, the unending squeeze and throb of her heart overrode every other aspect of her nondescript appearance. A dark dress was covered by a pelisse whose only nod to fashion lay in its military styled plackets down the front and in the trim of the sleeves.

An elderly gentleman stood at her side, his cravat almost obscured by whiskers. His features were composed of clear blue eyes, strong straight brows, and lean cheeks whose wrinkles revealed long years' worth of dimples such that he seemed to be perpetually in possession of a small smile. Despite their difference in years, it was evident that the young woman was his daughter. She retained his straight nose and brows, the piercing eyes, the full lips. Her hair, simply and practically dressed, was of a dark hue, indiscernible in the lighting, but it shone. Altogether, (though he did not contemplate it too deeply, he admitted) she was a handsome woman.

The woman's father paused to give them all a sad smile and nod before he allowed her to bring him around the circle of chairs to where two empty seats stood open.

John was aware that he was the only one surprised by her entrance. As it was his first time there, he was unaware what to expect. Perhaps the odd human in attendance was not abnormal. Why a human would attend a meeting for vampires was beyond his ken.

He watched surreptitiously from behind his glasses and couldn't help but feel some tension at her arrival.

Who was she? Expressing the depths of his struggles to one who had no experience with them was an acutely uncomfortable prospect. Perhaps he should just take his leave.

The chair to his right creaked in protest as his neighbor's much larger body maxed out its payload. He was a laborer by the look of him, and John was comforted at the thought that rank made little difference in regard to their suffering.

"'S 'right, cobba, she's a good 'un," the man whispered. 'Nary a sound or judgment from 'er. 'Ats her Da wiv 'er. Good man, yeah?"

The old man rose, drawing the attention of the room. No one, including the unsettling woman who sat across the way from him, was anything but compassionate.

"Good evening, friends. I'm so glad we were able to meet again. As you know, my name is Francis. Profession: Surgeon. I've been a vampire for six years, and haven't relied on human blood, willing or not, in three."

Everyone clapped. John's eyes ranged around the seated group of a dozen or so people – vampires all, save Surgeon Francis' daughter. Their pale clear faces reflected approval. Would he have the fortitude to stand up and make any admissions? He had never

8

taken anyone, but there were other things he wasn't proud of. Things that came about because he was a vampire. His eyes connected with the human across the room. For a moment he saw curiosity before her gaze dropped to her hands.

John adjusted his wire rimmed spectacles, fleeting annoyance passing over him at his vampiric deficiencies. He wouldn't care to go toe to toe with anyone present, even the speaker whose white hair and seeming frailty no doubt hid an unnatural strength. For the countless time, John cursed the day he had been attacked and changed.

"Recently, I have been having some… issues," Dr. Francis continued. His eyes met his daughter's. A shallow nod from her encouraged him to proceed. "Every day I become more tempted to partake. It becomes more difficult to resist. I was once able to get by on a gallon of ox blood every three days. Now I am up to a gallon a day. I fear…." His voice quavered.

The silence was absolute save for the woman's heartbeat. They all knew what it was he feared. A few nodded their heads in sympathy. The feeling that they had lost control to the desperate, wild hunger that ate at them unless their thirst had been satiated was a curse they all suffered at one point or another. John, too, felt a twinge of nausea. As far as diseases went, it was a truly gruesome one, when to give in to that unnatural temptation was to put one's soul in mortal peril. He must find a cure.

"Do you have someone helping you through this process?" Mr. Palmer, their host, asked. Without conscious thought Francis's eyes sought out his daughter's.

"Yes, I do."

"Excellent. If you ever require assistance, please be sure to let us know. After all, we intend to help each other learn to control our urges and live with this cross."

Francis nodded his thanks to the circle and took his seat next to his daughter. Mr. Palmer checked his watch.

"It appears we have enough time for one more before our hour is up. Is anyone else inclined?" His glance lingered on the only new member present. John shrank from the invitation. He wasn't ready for that kind of exposure. Maybe someday. But not today. He didn't feel he understood himself enough to be able to say anything.

A few minutes later the meeting dispersed. John hurried away from the Georgian fronted townhouse. He was ashamed to feel as if he were escaping the scene of a crime, but he wasn't comfortable with anyone recognizing him. Just in case there were rumors about Mr. Palmer's. It was possible. He didn't know anything about the man, other than that they didn't move in the same circles.

The hackney was still waiting for him around the corner as planned. After promising the driver twice the usual fee for his forbearance, he climbed in and the carriage pulled away into the quiet, lamp lit night.

John removed his spectacles and pinched the bridge of his nose in hopes of warding off the headache that threatened. It was the most absurd thing that despite his transformation, he suffered migraines and still had to fall back on his years of physical training to defend himself. No added strength, increased physical health, or unnatural speed for him. On the other hand, the sun did not burden him as it did most vampires.

Still, knowing what he knew – that vampires had acquired the benefits of the disease while he suffered only its ill effects – filled him with an undeniable envy. Other than the raging thirst for blood, the disease seemed to have little physiological effect on him. It was a curious fact. One he would like to explore more fully by experimentation, when he could.

Unfortunately his research had led him down a rabbit hole and he now had several different working theories regarding the almost impossibly small beings responsible for most of the world's deaths. On the other hand, this same rabbit hole of disease had provided him with a rich patron who had was extremely generous in providing what was necessary for his research.

Not that he needed the supplemental income.

If he only had an assistant to take care of beaker shipments, sanitize the lab, feed the rats, and arrange dishes, samples, and tinctures, he would have the time dedicate to such research.

John sighed. There were precious few people qualified to be his assistant, nor would he care to risk those few by exposing them to his disease. But even granting that he could acquire an assistant, his patron, Lord ----------, would hardly be impressed by a thesis explaining the disabilities of one abnormal vampire. Then again, would anyone?

The carriage rolled to a stop outside his modest Mayfair address. He paid the driver and let himself into the quiet house. He would have liked to have a butler standing there, ready to take his hat and cape. A valet to draw him a hot bath. A cook busy in the kitchens making tea.

As a vampire who had never needed to forgo his daytime habits, servants were a luxury he could ill afford. How would he explain his failure to eat? At one point, he had contemplated using the excuse that he dined out every day and didn't take a morning meal, but he didn't care to complicate his life. Even hiring vampire servants was out of the question since they were a trifle rare and, even so, were likely to be accustomed to night hours.

Not to mention, he thought as he released the catch on Maxwell's roomy cage, what servant in his right mind would be willing to put up with a pet rat, an eccentric master, and rooms taken over with an array of medical curiosities? No. Whatever desires he had to be taken care of were nothing compared to the mutual horror and fear that would take place should any human discover his sordid secret.

In the one cleared spot on the kitchen table, Maxwell stood on his hind feet and pulled at the slice of cheese John offered him. His white cheeks puffed out as he maneuvered the wedge around with nimble fingers, tearing tiny, rapid bites with his sharp front teeth.

When the rat was done, he cocked his snowy head again, whispers twitching. He was clearly asking for more. John shook his head. In his arrogance as a young medical student, he would never in a thousand years have envisioned that he would be envious of a rat's ability to enjoy cheese.

John took up the knife again and slid it down into the block. It was a pleasant feeling, to cut cheese. He could remember the anticipation of salivating over the rich, pungent smell of a hard wheel of local farmer's cheese. Now it was just a memory, not a sensation he could reasonably expect to feel again. Not without a cure.

He sighed and placed Maxwell back in his cage, slipping him another sliver to keep him happy. Despite his love for the rodent, he knew that if left unattended the creature would gorge himself. He checked the rat's water container and then trudged up the two flights of stairs to his suite.

A jumble of clothes lay on the floor of the dressing room. The counterpane from the bed appeared to be escaping via the window. The can of boot blacking sat open to the air from the morning.

Perhaps engaging a vampire man-servant, at least, was becoming a necessity. He imagined it would be more conducive to avoiding a mad dash out the door without his neck cloth or scorching yet another dress shirt while attempting to wield an iron.

John dropped onto the edge of the untidy bed to wrestle with his boots. He had a big day ahead of him on the morrow. His first job would be to visit the small farm he kept just outside of Town. His regularly scheduled feeding had to be done lest, with short warning, he turn into a raving lunatic and attack someone in the street. A cold shiver travelled down his spine at the thought.

****

Bracing fresh country air and the sound of song birds accompanied the first low rumblings of hunger. The country lane was infrequently travelled, being several miles from the nearest village of Fowlton and well off the beaten path.

His well-worn boots navigated crumbling wagon wheel ruts and baked horse droppings. He walked faster as the first pangs started to increase. His nose, one of the few sensible organs that had benefited from the disease, picked up on the earthy blood of wild animals in the hedgerows lining the lane. He wouldn't become desperate enough to chase one of them down before he reached the cottage. And he'd rather suffer the distance than be caught with a bloody mouth and a fresh kill by some wandering country folk.

He reached the private road that began his property and the hunger began in earnest – probably from the anticipation of a decent meal, he thought to himself. Five minutes later he was opening the door. The house was shadowed, the curtains pulled, but everything neat and clean. As always, he wouldn't linger. Despite the fact that he was the home's owner he always felt like he was intruding on another's privacy. Moses, the vampire he hired to care for his cattle, was an upstanding, simple man. He was now sleeping in the basement.

The strong smell of blood brought John to the kitchen. A fresh pitcher sat in the cooling tank, where rerouted spring water swept past and kept it chilled. His jaws began tingling. His mouth filled with saliva. He was tempted to drink straight from the jug, but that was hardly the act of a civilized man. Instead, he opened a cupboard and pulled out an earthen mug. He made himself move slowly and not give in to the desire to rush. But, finally, the cup was at his lips. The iron-rich tang of the thick fluid spilled down his throat, seeming to fill all those aching empty parts of him. He could almost see his cells and the spaces between them, filling with the blood. For a few minutes he experienced a heady rush of sheer power, the feeling that he could conquer the world. But it was so short-lived that by the time he had emptied the pitcher and drained the last mug of blood, he was full and lazy.

He rinsed his mouth out, and then the pitcher and mug. As per usual, he placed several coins on the counter for his servant and then left, in no hurry. He had several miles to walk before he would reach the country lane where he had left his hack. The walk invariably did him good. On feeding days, by the time he reached his laboratory on Griffin Street he could almost pretend he was normal. Never mind that the innkeeper viewed him with suspicion. He was, like many, an absentee landholder. But unlike other members of the gentry who wintered on their country estates, he regularly visited the cottage several times a week for all of a few hours. He knew they talked, that stories were starting to spring up about the cottage. It was cursed. It was haunted. Lights and shadows showed in the windows at night although it was supposed to be empty. Some of the village lads had come away stricken with terror after Moses had spooked them one night with some eerie moans when they were sure no one was at home.

John snorted to himself at the thought of them fleeing down the crooked lane. Were Moses a vampire of the usual type, they would have been right to be afraid. But he had hired Moses because the man didn't depend on human blood for sustenance. An old Scot, even before he was a vampire he was accustomed to drinking the fresh blood of sheep and cattle in the Highlands when food was scarce. And sure didn't Moses take a certain glee in sending shivers down the lads' spines.

John was in his laboratory before noon. The sun was truly up, the early morning fog long since chased away. Nevertheless, steam and smoke from the nearby factories left the air filled with haze. The familiar clanks and calls of the workers and drays making their way to and from the wharves and docks were a comfort to him. This was home. The center of his work. He gazed up at the narrow three story building with immense satisfaction before taking the steps up to the door three at a time.

The first floor of his laboratory was a warehouse given over to storing equipment. It wasn't a large space, but its rows of shelves were stocked with meticulous order, each shelf labeled and the contents covered with dust cloths. It was a far cry from his room at home.

On the second floor was a small drawing room, his office, and a bedroom holding a cot, a washstand, and a change of clothing – all in shabby repair. He stayed overnight more often than he felt he should, more than once finishing up with an analysis to discover the clock had struck midnight long before. But his office saw almost as much of him as his bed did. Between the research, the experiments, and notating his own findings, he was a very busy man.

He removed his coat and pulled on a canvas apron reserved for his experiments. One of a set he had cleaned twice a week, it was speckled over with fluid stains. He moved with banked excitement. The latest blood specimen, taken from a deceased dock worker, was proving to be fascinating. The man had died after a week long illness that included chills, vomiting, and intestinal issues. Unfortunately, he had not had the chance to treat the man, and so could only count upon the information provided him by the local apothecary who had intermittently attended him – when he was paid sufficiently. The symptoms were typical of a variety of illnesses, but no amount of being bled, applying hot stones to his feet, or ice baths had had any effect. The man finally died in his sleep after slipping into a coma. With reports that this was the fifth man to fall ill in this way, the locals of Old Nichol St. were becoming concerned that the plague was revisiting London. If he could discover how the disease grew and spread, they would have a better chance of saving lives.

Three days had passed since he had begun experimenting on several test rats. One of the rats was given a small laceration and the wound swabbed with the sample of diseased blood. Another had had a small amount of the blood mixed in with its food. Still another had the diseased blood painted onto the roof of its cage, which had then been shuttered in the hopes of discovering whether prolonged exposure to air would cause it to become contagious.

John went to his desk and reviewed his notes again. There had been no initial reaction. Four hours later there was still no significant change to the rat in

17

the shuttered cage. The rat with the skin laceration appeared to have localized redness and swelling. The rat with the poisoned food showed signs of digestive upset. As of yesterday, the symptoms had only been exacerbated in both of the affected rats. Today, he would see if the two affected were yet alive.

Journal in hand, John climbed the stairs to the third floor conservatory turned laboratory. Leaded panes of glass arched overhead and flanked both of the long sides of the room. Circular windows on each end shed more light into the room. One end of the room held the cages of rats. The other held washing stations while between them rows of tables held lab equipment.

John wrinkled his nose, and then adjusted his spectacles as he approached the cages. The smell alone indicated one or both of the affected rats was at death's door.

"Well, No. 347, how are we today, old fellow?" he asked as he pulled back the tarp covering the 3rd rat's cage. The rat rose to a standing position and grabbed hold of the bars of its cage, nose twitching. John began jotting down preliminary notes on the rat's condition. "Still alive and healthy, I see. Maxwell says hello. Lunch soon, eh?"

He moved on to the second one. The cage was fouled with bile and excrement. John was surprised to see what appeared to be blood smears. The rat was quite still, to the point that he could not quite determine whether it was dead. He leaned closer to the cage, but still detected no movement. Perhaps the creature had, in fact, died? Setting aside his journal he opened the cage and used a clean pair of tongs to pick the rat up. The protest was so faint he almost missed it, but protest there was.

John set the rat down again, excited at the prospect that one of his experiments was following the course of symptoms portrayed by the dock worker.

A quick check on the remaining rat showed a local infection around the incision, and a surly temperament, but nothing that indicated a similarity of condition to the deceased worker. He tossed the near dead rat into the incinerator and dumped the tongs into a vat of alcohol.

If the disease was food-borne, there was a possibility they could track down where the food came from and ask the owner to…. No, the grocer wouldn't be open to an inspection of his goods without the law to compel him. Of course, without the ability to identify the organism itself, he nor any other bacteriologist would be able to distinguish one food-borne illness from another, not without extensive testing.

And were word to get out that the grocer had introduced a contagion into the community, they were likely to pillory the man the next time someone fell sick, regardless of whether it was the same organism or not.

John fed the healthy rats, all the while contemplating the purchase of a microscope with a more powerful lens. The microscope he had simply wasn't powerful enough, even with the added advantage of the light. He had wanted the new equipment for years, and English craftsmanship wasn't on par with what the Germans produced. Now with the continent inaccessible due to the blackguard

Napoleon, it appeared that a new microscope would be far in the future – regardless of its imminent usefulness in testing his theories. With a more powerful lens, there might be a chance that he could see what made his blood different than that of the majority of other vampires.

He wasn't alone in his vampiric deficiencies. He had run into more than a few fellow-sufferers in broad daylight. Certainly, they were not common, and they had reacted to the sight of him with the same apprehension and fear as he had to them – as of one who has a terrible secret and is afraid he might be given away. If he could isolate what it was that made him different, it might help him discover a cure. It might be pure fancy or wishful thinking to suspect that his abnormal vampiric blood held the key to the cure, but he was sure there was some correlation.

He finished washing up and then went downstairs to organize his notes. Normally, he would finish his notes and then go up to work on something else, but with a Medico Society dinner planned for this evening, he could hardly risk running short of time and arriving late. He still had to return home, draw himself a bath, press a new shirt and cravat, and brush out his coat. With any luck, the preparation would take him two hours at most, at which time he could hire a hackney and make his way to Lord Waite's.

John rubbed his nose beneath his spectacles. It was dangerous attending parties that offered food. How long would it be before guests – friends – realized he never ate in their presence? The men were doctors, after all. How long would they accept the excuse that he had ongoing stomach troubles but yet appeared to be in the peak of health?

He closed the notebook with a snap and returned it to the drawer.

The prestige, company, and connections to be derived from attending such a function were well worth the stresses involved. That alone was enough to lure him away from his beakers and vials and skirt the danger of facing the overly inquisitive. If he had a manservant, it would require a great deal less effort.

****

Later that evening as he dressed, he contemplated what little he knew of his host. He had never met the man, but had received the invitation – a bold, strong hand on plain vellum – at the behest of a mutual friend and peer, Mr. Payard. The dinner was to be a large gathering of surgeons, physicians, and apothecaries, some of them fellows of the society, some not. He wondered whether there would be a single female present at the gathering. Regardless, he looked forward to a stimulating evening discussing the latest findings and techniques of those who were actually practicing. He, now working as a bacteriologist, did not practice at all unless it furthered his research. He didn't have the time, even if he had the inclination. Furthermore, he didn't dare risk putting himself in the position of being in contact with human blood on a regular basis. Who knew what would happen if he had to deal with a patient leaking blood all over the place? At least he could be grateful that his attack and subsequent change had come after he had completed his training at St. Bart's.

Finished with his ministrations, he stepped over to inspect his work in the mirror. He looked as much the gentleman as he knew himself to be. All without the aid of a valet. He would never be accused of aspiring to dandyism or being a Corinthian, but he didn't look shabby, which was all that mattered when one was attending dinner with a lord. To be sure it was an invitation most would envy, but he looked forward to it with some trepidation. He knew one lord, a viscount, who in his philanthropic interests had deigned to patronize his research. Now he was about to meet Alistair Murdock, the Earl of Waite. What had the man been told about him that would procure an invitation?

His hackney pulled up to the door of Waite's fashionable St. James' address. A butler answered the door and handed off his cape, hat, and walking stick to a waiting footman. He was conducted to a large drawing room decorated in somber hues and black-lacquered furniture. It was regrettable that he was the only guest yet present.

His host rose as he was announced. The earl had the neck and shoulders of a prize fighter while his stature topped John's own considerable one by a head and shoulders. The man's eyes were a flat black and unsettling in their unblinking perusal. But even had his physical attributes and serpentine gaze not intimidated John, the almost nonexistent rhythm of the earl's heart would have.

The earl was a vampire.

CHAPTER 2

John realized the earl knew him for what he was the moment he had crossed the threshold. They shook hands tensely. A moment of silent correspondence followed in which each acknowledged the unspoken awareness they had discovered.

The butler retreated, shutting the door behind them.

"Am I early?"

"Not at all." The earl's lips pulled back from his teeth in what John assumed must be his version of a smile. Was he attempting to set John at ease? It wasn't working.

"I sense you are uncomfortable," the earl continued. "I beg pardon. I had no idea you were one of us. I would have made sure to provide some sort of refreshment. If you'll give me a moment, I have a young woman who has volunteered herself for the purpose. I retain her services as needed. Just give me a moment."

The earl turned to pull the cord for the butler.

"No!"

His voice had come out more strained than he wished. Despite his aversion for such practices, he didn't care to show the earl how much he was disgusted by it. His host paused, eyebrows raised in question. "I am fully satiated. Thank you."

The earl came toward him again. "I will plead stomach ulcers and hope to avoid an onslaught of advice as to cures. What's your excuse?"

John shook his head. It figured that his host would have settled on the one excuse he had chosen.

"I'm particular about what I eat," he finally responded. "Or still suffering from a bout of tainted meat and my appetite isn't quite recovered."

Waite nodded.

"Do you smoke?" he asked.

"No. Thank you"

The earl went over to a small table where a collection of cigars, glasses, and a bottle of brandy stood at the ready.

"You are not early," he said as he clipped the end of a cigar. He lit the end with a match and put it out with a flourish. John refused to satisfy his curiosity by asking why he had been told to arrive earlier than the other guests. There was something about the man that raised his hackles.

"I was hoping to discuss something with you privately, before the rest of the guests arrived."

John waited.

"I have an interest in micro-organisms. And I hear you are a bacteriologist. That you are, in fact, going to present a paper to the Medico Society sometime in the near future. Is this correct?"

"Yes." An '*interest*'? John thought. What an odd turn of phrase. "Do you research yourself? I was not aware you had studied medicine at all."

"I may dabble in the study of medicine. But it's been years since I've practiced myself."

The bold statement filled John with questions. An heir apparent to an earldom didn't practice medicine, which either meant the earl was unexpectedly handed the earldom, or he was much older than he had let on and had acquired his fortune through means other than an inheritance. Waite was becoming more and more of an enigma.

"Is there anything in particular you wished to know?" John asked politely.

"Several, but it might be better if I set up an appointment. I thought perhaps I might stop by and visit your laboratory. If that is acceptable?" On the surface the phrasing of the words were polite, even friendly, but the latent demand came through clear as glass.

"I should be available any time this week. I usually keep regular hours, but find myself staying late more often than not."

"Regular hours?" The lord's brows lifted dramatically. "Daylight hours?"

"Yes. I'm what you would call 'immune' to sunlight."

"Interesting." He shrugged. "Today's Tuesday. Let's say Thursday evening. Eight o'clock?"

The door opened and the butler stepped in before John could make his reply. He nodded to Waite before the earl turned away to greet his new guests.

"Mr. Francis Isherwood and Miss Isherwood."

John was surprised to see the same elderly doctor who had attended the meeting at Mr. Palmer's the night previous. A flicker of recognition passed over his features as the introductions were made. Miss Isherwood, too, recognized him as faint blush and increased pulse indicated. All three men turned toward her in concern, but John noticed the earl's nostrils flaring, a feral look taking over his features.

"Miss Isherwood. A pleasure to meet you. Are you quite well?" John asked, determined to remind the earl that the young woman was a guest in his home with her father present. He didn't know enough about Waite to say whether the man would attack her, but he wouldn't put it past him to do so.

Her eyes connected with his. A hidden message – recognition of his efforts? – lay in their dark depths. Her gaze fell to his hand which still held hers and he became aware of those yet watching.

"Yes, of course. I am just over-heated," she said. She snapped open her fan and began fluttering it in the direction of her face as if to support the assertion.

"I am overjoyed you were able to bring your daughter, Mr. Isherwood. She will bring a welcome note of gentility and civilized rapport to the table tonight." John watched both Waite and Miss Isherwood as the smooth compliment came from the earl's mouth.

Mr. Isherwood, impatient with the talk of his daughter's supposed merits, nodded and pulled away from the earl.

"Starting early, today, aren't we, milord?" Isherwood asked with a wave to the cigar in Waite's hand.

"My apologies, my dear Miss Isherwood," Lord Waite said before stubbing out the cigar in a glass tray. "I would never had taken the liberty had I realized you were –"

"Oh no," she interrupted him with a laugh. "Father is just being cantankerous. In fact, I am fairly sure if you don't offer him one of your cigars, he may expire from desire any moment now."

Mr. Isherwood raised his gaze from his intent study of the cigars to rest it on his daughter.

"T'would be a blessing, I tell you, if I could expire."

"Father, I beg you will preserve my sensibilities. A happy discussion of your death is quite more than I could bear at the moment. And am I correct in imagining his lordship wouldn't appreciate a fainting damsel on his carpet?"

Lord Waite nodded from his position by the fire.

John kept silence throughout the exchange. He was amazed at Waite's pretense at politeness, and Miss Isherwood's seeming indifference to the danger she was in. She could not possibly be relying on her father's ability to defend her in the face of such a menace. But perhaps she was relying on his being a peer of the realm and expecting guests in a matter of moments? Or perhaps she was not fully aware of the danger Waite posed.

John continued to observe her as the remaining guests trickled in over the subsequent ten minutes. Almost all of them were known to him – fellow academics and parties interested in medicine or medical practice, though not all were doctors. A midwife and female herbalist helped to offset the predominantly male crowd, but the discussion yet centered on interesting cases in spite of the presence of the softer sex. Miss Isherwood's knowledgeable interaction and ease of manner in addressing the various members of the party intrigued him despite himself.

As he had expected, all of the guests were too taken up in their various discussions to bother with the formalities of rank. With some embarrassment (for it revealed to himself just how much he had been lurking) he found himself leading Miss Isherwood into the dining room. With her gloved hand on his arm, an unexpected warmth crept up his cheeks. He hadn't thought he was still susceptible to the fairer sex, cold-blooded creature that he was.

"What do you think, Mr. Grissom?" she asked as he seated her.

He was chagrined to realize he had lost the thread of the general conversation.

"Forgive me. I am not at the top of my form this evening, Miss Isherwood. Of what are you speaking?"

"The case Mr. Gervis took in Dartmoor with the mysterious illness. He is at a loss to explain it. I conjecture that there must be a common source, despite the fact that some of those who fell ill had no seeming contact with others who contracted the disease."

The first course was served. He could see from a clinical perspective that the dish would appear appetizing to the majority of the guests. It was a carrot soup. Utterly devoid of fresh blood, it was at best flat to his palate and could result in casting up his accounts were he to attempt its consumption. Nevertheless, for the sake of the other diners, he moved his spoon around and took some miniscule sips.

"Ah, yes. A most interesting case. But I have to believe there is a root cause for the disease, even if we remain unaware of what that cause is."

"Would you hazard a guess as to what?"

"Mr. Gervis ruled out water. I can only suppose we must rule out food since other family members didn't fall ill. But it is possible that the disease was transmitted via a carrier who had contact with both the family members and the other child who fell ill. And perhaps the period in which the organism's growth establishes itself varies from person to person. That would explain the timing of those who fell sick."

She paused, spoon halfway to her mouth.

"But wouldn't that mean the carrier was sick as well?"

"Unless he had acquired an immunity toward it."

She made a sound of skepticism.

"That still does not explain how it is contagious to some and not to others. I question the wisdom of ruling out exposure to a toxin or poison.

John was surprised. That had not crossed his mind.

"You think they were poisoned?"

"Mr. Gervis didn't mention the family had any known enemies, so there is no reason to suspect foul play, given the limited information he told us, of course. However, isn't it possible that the family members were exposed to something – a chemical or a gas – that sickened them, and the other little boy as well?"

John contemplated this new approach as his plate (as yet untouched) was cleared and the second course was served *en famille*. For politeness' sake he took a small serving of the stewed green beans and a thin slice of spiced pork. She looked at him sharply and then leaned in to speak in a low voice.

"Are you sure the dinner will agree with you?"

John paused, fork in mid-air. Did she disapprove of him? It wouldn't be unreasonable, considering what she knew. But no, her features only held concern for him.

"A full inquiry would need to be made in order to determine the cause," he said, after chewing down a sliver of the meat. "If such determination is possible at all. Were gypsies travelling through the area at the time, or in recent memory? Had they eaten certain foods that the others did not?"

"So, you insist on a correlation between the cases?" She relaxed, reassured by his nonchalance.

"I believe there must be a single contagion – or toxin – which is at fault. Whatever it is, it is deadly. I rue the fact that I cannot explore the region myself to determine how many other cases were reported of a similar nature."

Her glance fell on him again and she shook her head.

"I hardly think anyone in your position should risk exposing himself to other illnesses. My father, too, suffers as well you know. If he caught something from a patient, I hate to think what would happen to him."

John was puzzled.

"But the average, victim, let us say, has a propensity toward invincibility,"

"Or the seeming propensity. I am not in a position to study many of those who have fallen prey to the disease, but I am of the opinion that those who do store up, in a way, the effects of whatever illnesses they were exposed to but did not seem to contract."

John shuddered. It was hardly an encouraging analysis. But she had proved herself able to discern various aspects of medical practice without the benefit of formal training. An idea suddenly took hold. It was an idea that went against almost every demand of propriety, and the odds of her consenting to it were low, but he had to ask, and run the risk of her thoroughly cutting him for it. But first, he would need some understanding of her present position. It would take some delicacy to obtain the information without asking her outright. Then again, he never was a man for subtlety.

"Your father practices out of his home at the moment, is that correct, Miss Isherwood?"

"Yes, he does." Puzzlement rang in her voice at the abrupt change in conversation.

"And what do you intend to do when he is... no longer around?"

"To what do these questions tend, Mr. Grissom?"

"I only mean that without your father there to lend you countenance, you could hardly run the practice yourself. So...." John trailed off, his voice ending in a question.

Miss Isherwood stiffened and John realized he had provoked her too far.

"Forgive me." The words came out in an awkward rush. "I don't mean to intrude on your affairs. I am only concerned that a young woman of your intellect will find herself engaged as a governess, or worse, forced into an unequal marriage simply for lack of having a more – a more amenable situation."

She patted her lips deliberately with her napkin before folding her hands on her lap. She stared straight ahead, focused on the cascading floral centerpiece as if direct eye contact might give away more of her personal feelings on the matter than she wished to share.

"Mr. Grissom, despite any mutual problems we may have to face, I do not consider it good breeding to discuss my situation at table. Please do not count our solidarity in the face of the disease as more than it is."

John felt his neck suffuse with heat beneath his collar, the warmth reaching up to his cheeks.

"A thousand pardons. I am duly chastened." Chastened, but undeterred. He was determined to discover whether she would be open to his idea. "May I have the honor of calling upon you tomorrow afternoon? Perhaps we could take a walk?"

She turned to look up at him, skepticism evident in the arch of her brow. John held his breath in fear that he would be rejected. He firmly believed, very unscientifically, that no one else would be more aptly suited to his needs.

"Yes," she finally replied. "We're on Church Street. There is a square nearby."

Satisfied with her answer, he turned his attention back to pushing around his food. Around them lively debates and sharing of medical information and news abounded. Many of them had mutual acquaintances and similar interests so it was not hard for the conversation to flow freely.

"How is your research coming along, Mr. Grissom?" Lord Waite asked from one seat down at his end of the table. "Mr. Payard informed me you enjoy the patronage of a viscount. What does your research entail?"

"I perform extensive testing on the properties of blood," John said. He paused and met the man's eyes in an unspoken exchange before continuing. "But the majority of my efforts are made in the attempt to discover the source of various contagions. I am convinced if we were able to discover the most common carriers of disease, it would be of great aid in eradicating contagions and containing epidemics."

"It sounds like many hours spent peering into a microscope."

"Indeed, it is. But what I am able to do with the one I have is quite limited. I hope to acquire a new one, but with the war, German manufacturers haven't been accessible."

"German?"

"I regret to say, our native craftsman lack the ability to produce lenses powerful enough to see what I would like."

Waite stroked the stem of his wine glass, deep in thought.

"We'll have to discuss these German lenses more at length on a later date."

John nodded. Although Waite was interested in the medical field, he must be a peculiar individual to discuss the various aspects of microscope lenses. It was hardly a fascinating study to one unfamiliar with the details.

Because of the singular company, whose main interest lay less in impressing each other with their social acumen and more with sharing information, the party adjourned to the drawing room in short order. The ladies gallantly allowed the men their cigars and brandy, with the caveat that all the windows be opened, along with the French doors.

John had stepped out for a breath of fresh air and to clear his head when the muted sound of voices from a room situated further down the terrace met his ears.

Like his sense of smell, his hearing was more acute than the average. He was starting to suspect that it was even more so than that of the average vampire – a circumstance he found at odds with his other less than exemplary vampiric talents.

"When did you leave them?"

It took him a second to place the voice. Lord Waite. Truly, John wasn't attempting to eavesdrop, but it was hardly avoidable while he was taking the air.

"Three nights ago. Unfortunately, they began the inoculations ahead of schedule." The second man's voice contained a trace of Scots.

Silence reigned for several beats.

"So none of the troops received the new serum?" Rage was thinly veiled in the earl's controlled tone. John leaned forward, now intent on hearing the remainder of the conversation.

"No, my lord."

"I'll have to demand a mandate to do them over again."

"Perhaps they were improperly prepared? I could infect several of them with a different contagion. If you can send in one of your apothecaries, they could investigate and confirm that the inoculations didn't take."

"Yes. Do it. Our Regent won't know the difference. He won't question my recommendations."

"I should think not! You're the head of his Physiological Development. If he only knew what the French receive – "

"Shut up. Do you forget we have guests?"

The voices dropped in volume making it impossible for John to hear without approaching closer. But he didn't dare risk proximity. Not with a powerful vampire. What he had overheard was alarming news indeed. He had never heard of such a government agency as Physiological Development. Of course, it stood to reason that with a war going on, the government would consider every possible avenue of attack – of which disease was definitely a powerful one. But it was dreadfully awkward if he had stumbled in on a conversation that was intended for the ears of King's men only.

John lingered in the doorway of the drawing room, reviewing the conversation in his mind. Three days. Three days travel from London likely meant the Continent, if one assumed swift travel. But in order to falsely inoculate French troops within three days? That would mean being able to get through the French lines – with inoculations – with relative ease. Smugglers? Possible. On the other hand, it occurred to him that there was no reason to assume, as he had, that Waite's man had come from the French. The thought sent his pulse racing, or half-way to normal, as it were.

Three day's travel could mean he came from the North. It could mean Wales. One needn't even go that far. He shook his head, disconcerted at the conclusion he had to draw. The troops they were discussing must be British. They were being exposed to a disease of some sort. And they had missed the exchange of the good inoculations for the disease that Waite had cooked up.

Whatever it was, he could only speculate that the dormant period was a long one. It wouldn't be toward the purpose to "inoculate" the soldiers, only to have them show up sick the next day. But if his conjecture was correct, Waite was a spy of the worst sort. With an ear to the highest, if one of the most foolish, powers in the land.

"What are you pondering on so deeply, Mr. Grissom?" A female voice interrupted his thoughts. Miss Isherwood stood near him, her arm linked through Mr. Gervis'. The man was almost as old as her father, but he fleetingly wondered whether Mr. Gervis had marital intentions. John shoved the thought away.

Why had it even arisen?

"Your case, Mr. Gervis," John said, nodding toward the man. "Most unusual. Do you frequently encounter such?"

"No. Like every other country surgeon and physic, I am inundated with commonplace ailments: gout, fevers, megrims, the list goes on, and is as much a bore."

John thought a moment. What he had learned about Lord Waite had his mind flipping in different directions. Physiological Development. What were they developing? Strains of a disease? A new strain? Of what? A cold knot formed in his stomach. It almost reminded him of the hunger for food he used to be able to feel.

"Do you suppose a person, say, a Frenchman, could infiltrate our country and release a disease into an area?" John asked.

Mr. Gervis arched a brow at him. Miss Isherwood waited on Mr. Gervis' response.

"Unlikely. I don't see how a person would be able to control it without risking infection himself," Mr. Gervis said.

"Can such diseases not be contained in metal or glassware?" Miss Isherwood asked.

"They could, given the proper equipment," Mr. Gervis said. "I wouldn't put it past the French to make the attempt."

Miss Isherwood shook her head.

'No, I don't believe it's likely. Not in this case."

"Why is that?" John asked.

"First, I don't believe the French situation allows for equipment of the caliber such an undertaking would require. Second, if the French were going to attempt to reintroduce – let us say, the Black Plague – "

"May all the saints preserve us!" Mr. Gervis said fervently.

"I believe they would introduce it in a heavily populated area. London, for example," she said.

John nodded. It made sense. As much as he would like to paint Lord Waite the villain with as thick a brush as possible, introducing a disease into a small populated area would hardly serve to create havoc.

"Unless it was a test group," Miss Isherwood continued after a moment.

John raised his head. Why hadn't he thought of that? Of course the man had to test on someone. Rats wouldn't be as reliable as live humans.

"She thinks like a medico," John said to Mr. Gervis. The man chuckled.

'Does it intimidate you?" she asked. A blush stained her cheeks as if she realized it was a forward question.

"Not at all. The day women have the opportunity to train along with us will be the day modern medicine increases its life-saving abilities by leaps and bounds. Being more sensitive and intimately familiar with the inner-workings of a household must give them greater advantage than someone like myself."

"Doing it much too brown, Grissom," Gervis said with a grin. "Miss Isherwood is immune to your flattery. She needs no convincing of your abilities. She was discussing them with me not moments ago."

"And now you tell tales out of school, Mr. Gervis. For shame!" She rapped him on the arm with her fan before turning back to John. "I was given to understand from Lord Waite that you research diseases of the blood."

"Sturdy as they come. No fainting lily here," Mr. Gervis said with approval.

"As you know, Mr. Gervis, my father is not in the best of health," she said. "He requires assistance in his rounds on occasion. Swooning would hardly help our situation."

"Practical too!" Mr. Gervis crowed.

"Do you know Lord Waite well, then?" John asked. If she did, perhaps cultivating a friendship would give him some insight into the earl's secret activities.

"No. He and my father are friends. Since before I was born, I believe, for all that Lord Waite doesn't look a day over 45. He is a frequent dinner guest, however."

"I hazard to say it's not just milord's friendship with her father that is such a draw," Mr. Gervis winked.

"Any more from you, and I will find another gentleman to take my arm," she said in mock admonishment. "Do be kind. Mr. Grissom was just going to tell us of his findings on blood related diseases."

"I was?" John asked, surprised out of his listening to their banter.

"Oh. Weren't you?" Her voice was full of disappointment.

"I would hate to bore you, Miss Isherwood. My findings can be quite pedantic. No doubt nothing like what you are used to."

Miss Isherwood laughed and turned to Mr. Gervis.

"Mr. Grissom obviously does not know my father."

Mr. Gervis shook his head admiringly.

"This young woman manages to stay awake through discussions which have even my eyes glazed over."

"So you were saying, Mr. Grissom?" Miss Isherwood prompted. John could not but be flattered at her show of interest. He was convinced of its sincerity by the look in her eye, but also by his knowledge of what her father was, and the fact that she had admitted the man was ailing. It was an unfortunate circumstance, but one that might prove to his advantage. Reason after reason rose in support of the proposition he would make to her tomorrow.

He could only hope her sense of propriety was not so refined that it would prohibit her from considering what he had to offer.

CHAPTER 3

John resisted the urge to press his face against the eye piece, knowing that it wouldn't help him to view the blood cells any closer. His darkened cells didn't appear to be reacting to the dead blood cells of the dock worker. Nor were the free floating staffs surrounding his cells penetrating. He had yet to discover why it was that vampires were immune to most diseases, but this confirmed they were resistant on a microscopic level.

He pulled away from the microscope and rubbed his forehead with his arm. The pieces of glass holding his sample went into the "To Wash" bin, and then he washed his hands. He would have to make sure he was doubly careful with his specimens if he was going to introduce a non-vampiric assistant into the lab, as he hoped.

A glance at his watch revealed that his rendezvous with Miss Isherwood was fast approaching. He pocketed it and grabbed up his coat. If he walked at a fast pace, he would make it before noon. He couldn't imagine that she would be adverse to a morning call. The Season was in full swing, but doctor's daughters weren't in the habit of mingling with the Ton. In theory, she would have had an early night, which made a morning call acceptable.

He arrived with minutes to spare. It was a modest, older home with a door in need of repair and a well-worn brass plaque inscribed with the words *Mr. Francis Isherwood, Surgeon*. He was surprised to be met by the lady of the house herself – though he didn't know what he had expected. After all, it was the home of vampire and servants could be liabilities as much as they could be aides. She appeared at the door in a crisp white apron and rather wilted mob cap, her jonquil striped morning gown protected by white over sleeves. Her heart rate increased at the sight of him. He tried not think about it.

"Miss Isherwood!"

"Good morning, Mr. Grissom." She held the door open for him. "Do come in. Give me just a moment and I'll join in you in the drawing room."

She opened the doors to an airy bright room on the first floor.

While he waited, he studied several watercolor landscapes, which, by their amateurish hand and the initial H. Isherwood, he supposed to have been completed while she was yet in the school room.

He turned at the sound of a step at the door. She re-entered having changed her dowdy cap for a much more becoming bonnet trimmed with pale yellow roses, and the apron for a pink pelisse. At his perusal, she lifted a gloved hand to her cheek.

"No errant blood spatters, I hope?"

"No." He cleared his throat. "You must ascribe to the notion that a pleasing picture aids healing."

"Oh, that old thing?" she laughed, waving at the painting he had stepped away from. "No, our patients wait in a different room."

"I was… I was referring to your," he sketched a hand down his body.

"Oh! My ensemble! Why, thank you for that kind compliment, Mr. Grissom. The patients have been piling up this morning so if I am acceptable for a walk in the park without changing my entire outfit, it's pure luck."

"Are you in the habit of answering the door yourself, then?"

She shook her head.

"No. Visitors don't usually knock. I have a desk I sit at in our waiting room. Then, if my father is unavailable, I begin recording their symptoms."

"I take it you are of great aid to your father. You seem capable."

She busied herself tying the ribbons on her bonnet.

"I am the fortunate daughter of a doctor who has an appreciation for my intellect."

"Some would object to exposing females to what a doctor experiences."

She blew air out of her mouth and moved on to buttoning her gloves.

"We are the gentler sex, I grant you, but women are as intellectually capable of practicing medicine as men. There will come a point in time when we will be able to obtain training and a license to practice, I am sure of it."

He smiled and bowed from the waist.

"And if there are many women as dedicated in their intent as you are, I have no doubt they will make worthwhile surgeons."

"If only my patients would agree with you. Generally, they believe that because I am a woman, I am incapable of offering the most basic remedies. They always ask for my father."

"Regrettable, but, as you say, it will change in time. Should I pay my respects to your father, do you think?"

"If you like. He isn't able to see as many patients as he would like because of his illness, but I'm sure he won't object to meeting with you."

He followed her through the house to the back door which lead onto a shallow terrace overlooking a small rose garden. Mr. Isherwood sat in a chair by the rail, but started to rise at the sight of a guest.

"I beg you, sir, do not stand on my account. I only wished to pay my respects before I accompany your daughter on a walk."

Mr. Isherwood settled himself again, relief evident on his face.

"You remember Mr. Grissom from Lord Waite's dinner, do you not, father?" Miss Isherwood asked.

"Girl, I might be suffering from ailments of the stomach, but my mind remains unaffected. I remember him from more than just Waite's dinner. He was at Maynard's meeting." Mr. Isherwood proffered John a hand. "Good sir. We didn't have the chance to talk much at Waite's, but I was surprised, if not to say glad, to discover another vampire practicing medicine."

John laughed.

"I don't know if it could be said that I practice. My contributions to the health of patients takes a less immediate approach."

"Valuable work, nevertheless. The more we know about contagious diseases, the easier it will be to combat them. Jenner is doing some work experimenting with inoculations. The dairy maids never catch smallpox and he figures it must be because of their exposure to cow pox. Who knows what will come of it?"

John's ears perked up. Had Lord Waite discovered Jenner's technique and replicated it? If he was the head of some sort of secret governmental organization for advancing the soldier, it made sense that the army would receive the first round of inoculations. Secretly, if nothing else.

"But we could discuss such things all day," Mr. Isherwood resumed. "You came to take Henrietta for a walk. Let me warm myself in the sun here while you are gone."

John inclined his head and Miss Isherwood kissed her father's cheek. John followed her winsome figure between the adjacent house and her own and out a connecting side gate.

"Now, the square on Church St. is all of two blocks away," she said as she took his arm. "If we amble, it will take us ten minutes to walk there."

"Rushing back so soon, Miss Isherwood?"

She raised her face to the sun, lifted her shoulders and smiled up at him.

"No. Most emphatically, no. It has been too long since I've had the opportunity to enjoy a walk in the park. To enjoy the little things outside my own sphere of experience. My father's increasing ill health means that he requires more care. And to make matters more worrisome, many of our patients have begun seeing other surgeons, even if they are far away."

"Does that not cause problems with your current situation?"

Miss Isherwood drew herself straighter than she stood already.

"We will manage, Mr. Grissom. Our income is not so straightened, yet, that we have cause for anxiety."

Her glance fell on him and softened. "I do appreciate the concern, however. It is a welcome change to have someone else personally concerned for my father's welfare."

John coughed to cover his embarrassment. If she only knew his self-serving motives. He winced. It would probably be best to bring up those motives now. But carefully.

"May I ask when your father contracted the disease?"

"Do you mean, when was he attacked?"

John nodded.

"I was seventeen at the time. We used to live in -- ---------shire, in a cottage outside of R--------, a small hamlet. It was essentially in the country, though only a half day's ride into Town. He was called to the bedside of a young man who had lost a great quantity of blood and had fallen into a coma. As night fell, the young man began to stir and rave. He became so unsettled that my father grew concerned.

He realized the young man would need to be restrained, but the rage – madness – came over him so quickly he couldn't restrain the man himself. He sent the widow for reinforcements. While she was gone, the young man overcame him. They knocked the lamp over in their struggle. He couldn't see anything, but the man seemed to have an inerrant knowledge of where he was.

Of course, we know now what senses are enhanced in those so afflicted. The last thing he remembers before falling into a faint was being grabbed and feeling something pierce his neck. The next morning, I was sent for. The young man was gone, the home in shambles, and my father, to uneducated eyes, was dead with two puncture wounds in his neck. I took him home and prepared –"

"No hue and cry? Why wasn't the coroner called for, an inquest performed?"

"The locals were terrified. My father was dead, killed by a raving madman. No one saw the purpose of it. I wanted to grieve for my father and the widow was distraught over not knowing what had happened to her son. The young man never resurfaced."

"How long until your father… turned?"

Miss Isherwood searched the sky as if the answer lay somewhere in the clouds.

"It must have been no more than two nights when he began to stir. I was in the barn, settling our animals for the night.

I had yet to write to my uncle and inform him his only brother had died. The funeral was set to be performed the next day. I had many things weighing on my mind.

The scraping sound of feet on the dry grass path leading to the barn drew my attention. My father lurched into view, looking like death itself. I had cleaned him up by then and dressed him in his burial suit so he didn't look gruesome from blood, but from his pallor.

Nothing can prepare one to see a corpse go walking around, father or not. He paused at the doorway and I ducked my head behind a stall, hoping he wouldn't notice me. There was a scuffle and then the braying of a cow at its last prayers. I risked a glance only to discover my father latched onto the neck of the animal and drawing deep gulps as if he were starving.

There were no words for my fright. I snuck away into the night as quickly and quietly as possible."

Miss Isherwood fell silent. He didn't want to interrupt her fear-filled memories and so continued their slow amble.

"Eventually I found my way to my uncle's town house. I didn't have the heart to tell him what had occurred with my father, just that he was dead. I didn't know what to think of what I had seen. So many questions would go unanswered for there was no one in whom I could confide. As night approached on the third day after my escape, there was a thump at my window. My nerves were greatly overset as you can imagine, but I was determined not to live in terror of every errant bird or tree branch.

I approached and flung back the curtain, only to see my father standing on the ledge outside, looking very much himself and not at all the gruesome, punctured, dead creature he had been only days before. I screamed, but my uncle was not at home to hear it and my room was set up far from the servant's quarters. He made the most sincere gestures of fatherly love and concern that I could not but doubt what I had witnessed in the barn. Nevertheless, I refused to allow him entrance and eventually he went away much saddened.

The following day, my uncle accompanied me to Hatchard's. As we left, my father hailed us on the street. My uncle almost died of an apoplexy of happiness at the sight of him, but, naturally, I was much more reserved. I could not imagine, however, that he would be so crazed as to attack us in full view of the busy street, so I expressed my amazement and concern for this change of events.

He made it clear that he expected us to resume the life we had shared, but in London. My uncle invited him home for dinner that night. Later, my father sought me out and gently explained to me the gruesome facts of his existence, to the extent that he understood it. He assured me that he would only feed on animals and would never put me in a position wherein I should fear for my safety. And he never has." Miss Isherwood sighed and turned to smile up at him. "And that is tale of Mr. Francis Isherwood, Surgeon."

"Not quite all. I beg you will forgive my overweening curiosity, Miss Isherwood, but as one interested in pathology, I find your father's condition – illness – given his vampirism, to be unusual. I know it is terribly forward of me, perhaps unforgivable, to question you on it. My research is not solely directed toward discovering more information about micro-organisms, but also toward discovering a cure for vampirism. I believe it to be the product of a disease. Like him, I am not a typical vampire. I must wear spectacles to see clearly. I haven't the speed or strength they are known for. I do have superb hearing and smell, and I can obviously withstand daylight, but that is the extent of any positive side effects of my disease."

"A chronic disease, then? But does a disease not kill?"

John heaved a sigh.

"I suspect I am dead already. Or almost. If that makes sense. My heart beats but barely. Something like ten times a minute. My blood cells are darkened almost to the point of blackness. The vampiric existence is altogether irregular."

"I don't understand. If that is so, then wouldn't it be impossible to make a recovery?"

"Mostly dead might be just enough alive to pull through," he said with wry humor.

"My father told me of a case wherein a man who lived through a vampire bite did not end up turning, but his mind broke. They become mad who survive it and don't turn."

"This is new to me. I should like to speak with your father on the subject in greater depth. Do you suppose he would mind?"

"Not at all." She shook her head. "He's very open about his condition, at least to those he counts as friends."

John didn't have that luxury, but he did have hopes that Mr. Isherwood would consider a closer collaboration. And if his daughter would accommodate him....

"I wonder-" John paused, searching for a way to approach the prickly question.

"Yes?" She ceased walking, and looked up at him, her hand on his arm.

"Please," he waved toward the park entrance mere steps away. A few gentlemen with ladies on their arms strolled on the graveled pathways, but the two of them could continue to speak in relative privacy as they walked.

"I have a proposal for you, Miss Isherwood, and there is just no good way to say it."

Her eyebrows rose almost to her hairline. John realized how what he said could sound.

"Allow me to rephrase my poorly chosen words. Ahem. I am in need of an assistant, a laboratory assistant, to help me in my research. I have not family. I have not cultivated the friendship of any vampires, and I cannot depend on the friendships of my non – I do so hate to throw the word vampire around so loosely. One never knows who might be listening. Do you object to my calling them Afflicted (and we shall understand it to mean vampirism)?" At her nod, he resumed. "As I say, I cannot rely on my non-*Afflicted* friends because the nature of the work must needs reveal my affliction."

"So assistant is not code for ladybird?"

John gasped at her bald question.

"Good heavens, no!"

Her face fell. "Oh!" she said. She almost sounded disappointed, but he couldn't fathom why.

"What is it?" he asked.

"Nothing. Nothing at all," she declared, though her face and voice clearly revealed to him that it was far from nothing. "Go on, sir. You were saying, about an assistant? Do you need a recommendation, then?"

"Why, no. I had rather hoped…" he trailed off. She would pick up on what he was trying to say, wouldn't she?

"Yes?"

"You, Miss Isherwood! I was rather hoping you would consider applying for the position. You will receive a monthly stipend of 20£. Please tell me that at the very least you will give it due consideration."

"25£ and I'll think on it," she said with a sly look.

"Miss Isherwood, I really must protest," he said with mock severity as he adjusted his spectacles higher on his nose. "25£! That's extortion!"

"Didn't you mention to Lord Waite that you have a wealthy patron? He would so appreciate how much more time you have, he'll be happy to pay the 25£."

" I should take you with me next time I visit Bond Street, Miss Isherwood, I am sure you could finagle the price for my cravats to a lower figure. Speaking of Lord Waite," he interjected, though they had not been speaking of Lord Waite at that moment at all. "How familiar are you with the man?"

"Not familiar with the man at all, beyond a passing acquaintance. Just what rumor says."

"Which is what?"

They had left the park and were now strolling toward her house, albeit at a slower pace than when they had set out. She stopped and looked up in surprise.

"Mr. Grissom, I would not have expected one who was so mannerly to request that I repeat unsubstantiated rumor."

"Yes, those are the worst kind," John said. "I myself prefer the substantiated rumors. One feels more justified in spreading them."

"Insufferable man!" she said, continuing to walk.

"Yes, well, it was either I quiz you on Lord Waite, or I depend on a cloak and dagger routine I would just as soon avoid."

"But I don't understand. Why?"

"I have my reasons, but suffice it to say, I daren't give voice to my suspicions until I have some assurance that they can be proved. Nevertheless, I will say, information on Lord Waite could prove crucial to saving London, perhaps even England itself."

She arched a skeptical brow at him.

"Come, Mr. Grissom, what could Lord Waite possibly do to pose so dramatic a threat? It sounds like the veriest Banbury tale and I can tell you I am not easy prey to being played the fool."

"I assure you, Miss Isherwood, I wish I were exaggerating, but if what I – well, never mind. If you have any faith in my ability to be objective, I hope you will realize that I could not be more serious."

Her silence following the pronouncement was a thinking one. No doubt, the kind, gentle, spectacled doctor had scared her with his talk of gloom and doom.

"I am almost home," she finally responded. "Were you anyone less than who you are, I confess, I would assume you are trying to cause trouble. Yet, I cannot help but believe you are sincere. Nevertheless, things are never as they seem.

Both my father and I were surprised to receive his invitation, but after we realized the earl was, er, *Afflicted*, we assumed our company was preferred by him for comfort or fraternity's sake. I cannot imagine the occasion will be repeated. Either way, I have not much of import to share.

We have gleaned that he works for the Crown in some capacity. His medical interest could be no more than a stimulating pastime, but I am convinced it is harmless."

Her words echoed in the far corners of his mind. 'He works for The Crown.' That confirmed his earlier suspicions.

They came to a stop outside her door.

"Is he really so dangerous, do you think?" she asked, one hand on the handle.

"I don't know. Good evening, Miss Isherwood. Please think on my offer. Your help would be invaluable."

"No guarantees, mind you, Mr. Grissom. But it does sound exciting. With my father's business dwindling, the steady income will be a welcome boon. But, we will see. My father may voice objections I did not consider."

Moments later, she was enclosed within. John walked a full twenty feet toward Griffin St. before he realized he was whistling a tune.

CHAPTER 4

John almost trod on the man's velvet dancing pumps. He stumbled back down the steps taking in the snowy folds and high shirt points that framed the face belonging to the very person he had been discussing with Miss Isherwood the morning before. Lord Waite's hair was slicked back with perfumed oil, but in the darkened light of night, offset by his pale complexion and his powerful physique clothed in full evening dress, the earl looked devilish. And lit with a cold fire, if his near-glowing cat-like eyes were any indication.

"Preoccupied this evening, Mr. Grissom?"

The words sounded innocent enough, but John felt they were a rebuke.

"Yes, actually," John replied, heading up and around the earl to get to his door. "It's busy days at my laboratory."

Lord Waite followed him inside. Though John was disgruntled by the lord's presumptions, he couldn't very well object to it. So instead he took the older vampire's hat, cloak, and cane, and led him into the front drawing room. He lit the fire and several candles and turned to hunt up some brandy.

"No need, thank you." Waite remained standing, looking about the room with what could only be curiosity. "This is a comfortable place. I'm surprised you don't keep servants to see after the upkeep. And your appetites."

Was the man probing? John removed his spectacles and wiped them down with his handkerchief as he contemplated an answer. This man, he intuited, was dangerous. He needed to discover how and why, if England's soldiers were indeed being involved in whatever plan the head of the Physiological Department was dreaming up.

"My needs are take care of," he replied. "You weren't waiting long?"

The topic change didn't throw his lordship at all.

"No longer than I thought it worth."

John leaned an arm against the mantle in a casual pose that was entirely feigned. Waite would arrive at the purpose of this interview. Was he waiting for encouragement from him? Interest?

"I trust your diners professed no concern over their host's lack of appetite the other evening?"

"No, they never do." His smile was devoid of warmth. "They are all of them ignorant. Weak. Vulnerable. Do you despise them?"

"Me?"

"Especially you. You know how weak and mewling they really are. Granted," he twitched a finger in the direction of John's face, "you are somewhat deficient yourself as far as the Blood Gifted goes. But, I'm willing to forgive it."

"Are you," John said, deadpan. He didn't know what game Waite was playing it, but the man was starting to sound like a fanatic. And what was the 'Blood Gifted'?

"We have a project going on which could use your skills and knowledge-"

"We?"

"The formal members of a brotherhood made up of vampires."

"That would be this Blood Gifted group?"

"No. All vampires, whether they know it or not are one of the chosen ones, but we, my brothers and I, actually acknowledge it."

"Is this an invitation then?"

"If you like. Your expertise will certainly further our cause."

"Which is?"

Waite stood with his hands clasped behind his back. His close perusal from the onset of their conversation had proved more and more unsettling. But John forced himself to ignore the man's narrow eyed gaze and lounged in a wing-back chair before the crackling fire.

"You will forgive me if I don't believe we have attained a level of trust commensurate with sharing such information."

"What can I do for you then, my lord?" John asked, finally having lost his patience.

Lord Waite began to pace about the room, gathering his thoughts as he spoke them.

"We know vampires are immune to disease, but we don't know why. Is it possible that were we to isolate whatever compound is found in the blood's serum, we could manufacture cures specific to certain diseases. Do you think it possible?"

John raised his eyebrows in surprise. A cure. When he had first discovered Waite on his doorstep, he was afraid that the man would attempt to strong arm him into some nefarious scheme. But a cure?

"Before you answer, I can tell you that we already have a small sample of the serum available that we would like to use. We were hoping you could study it, attain more vampiric blood and create more serum. After that, we hope to determine what the exact compound is that makes vampires invulnerable to disease. In exchange, other than the obvious part of being something groundbreaking, I can offer you the lens you were hoping to get from Germany."

"Why?"

"I think it's only fair that we offer to compensate you for-" Waite began.

"Why do you want to come up with a cure for these ills?"

"I believe it is our obligation as one of the Blood Gifted to use what we have for the betterment of humanity."

Waite's philanthropic motivations were so surprising as to be questionable. As was the readiness of his answer.

But cures for dyspepsia, typhoid, tuberculosis, cholera, and consumption were cures nonetheless.

"Where did the original serum come from?"

A frisson of anger rippled across Waite's face before he regained the cold mask he normally wore.

"I am afraid that is not pertinent to the matter at hand."

Which meant, John thought, it was probably something involving death and the Crown – or perhaps Waite just wanted it to stay secret. John pinched the bridge of his nose beneath his spectacles. He had the feeling this entire episode was going to result in a lot more effort on his part than he was desirous of giving at this point in his life. It would be so much easier to ignore all those pesky objections of conscience, to damn nobility and honor in favor of his research and the prestige of crafting something so potentially pivotal to the development of medicine.

"I need to think about it," John said.

Waite nodded.

"Understandable. Don't wait too long to let us know what your intentions are. We would hate to run another vampire medico to ground, but I suppose it could be done."

John snorted.

"Doubtful, my lord. As far as I know, I am the only one of my breed."

"Then you are doubly gifted," Waite said, holding out his hand.

John grasped it and shook. The earl pumped his hand once with an iron grip. "I'll see myself out."

The door closed behind him and John sat staring into the flames. The truth was, he couldn't deny what he had overheard. And yet he didn't trust the earl. There was some havey-cavey business going on with the inoculations for the army regulars. And somehow France was involved. No man interested in the health of humanity would consider purposely infecting soldiers for the sake of forcing through an emergency "inoculation." He would have to discover more information before he agreed to take part in anything.

****

John left the stables after his thrice weekly trip to the cottage. Once again, he was full and sated. He looked forward to a day spent in the lab. And perhaps some sleuthing. He couldn't very well call in Bow Street about his suspicions in regard to the earl when it would advertise the existence of vampires. The ensuing riots would rival the Luddites for damage.

He had thought about his options long and hard the night before, the lengths he would go to discover the truth behind what he had overheard. In the wee hours of the morning, his conscience fully wrestled with, he had put aside his fears and excuses – of which there were many – and decided to spy on the earl. He didn't yet know what sort of risks that would entail, or how much time it would take away from his work, but having committed himself to the cause, he wasn't about to let that stop him. It was relieving in a way. The indecision of whether or not to act no longer hung over him like a black cloud.

He wasn't quite up for whistling this morning, but with the hope that supposition would supply for his lack of positive humor, he started in on a rambling tune as he turned the corner onto Griffin St. The sound died on his lips at the sight of the somberly dressed woman waiting on the steps, a book open on her lap.

Miss Isherwood. John pulled out his watch. 11 o'clock. How long had she been waiting? He sped up his pace.

Her head rose as he approached and a relieved smile spread across her cheeks.

"Mr. Grissom! Did you wake up late this morning?"

"No, no. I, er, had to go get breakfast."

She took a step back.

58

"Nothing… human, I hope?"

"No. I may have the temptation, but I am not that sort of beast."

Her shoulders relaxed.

"Have you been waiting long?" he continued as he let her into the building and divested himself of his cape and cane.

"About a half hour. It took some doing to discover where your laboratory was located, but Lord Waite was happy enough to supply us with the information when he called on my father early this morning."

He stashed her pelisse and reticule on a bench in his office and then led the way up the stairs to the laboratory.

The monkeys began screeching at him for their food and a furor of activity met his ears as typically happened when he entered the room.

"Pardon the noise. Lord Waite?" John was surprised the man was making himself so familiar with the Isherwoods. He didn't seem the type to call on one for fraternity's sake.

"Yes. It was an unexpected visit, if convenient for me. He came before the sun was up. I'm sure you can imagine why he came at that hour."

"I can't say I like the idea of Waite becoming friendly with your father. Not that it is any of my concern." John clapped his hands and spun in a circle, presenting the room. "Well, as you can see, here is where I do my research. My office is downstairs. Equipment at the front, experimental test animals at the back. Unfortunately, I wasn't expecting you so soon, but if you are as competent as I imagine you to be, it should not make a difference."

"Should I come again at a later date?" She lifted labeled vials he had lined up in a tray. "I had assumed there was some urgency."

"So there is. Especially now. I find that I have… another project I must undertake. It will take me away after the sun goes down and late into the night. My working periods will change because of it, but the sunlight is essential to view anything through the microscope, so I will have to come in the mornings as often as I can. I can't ask you to work past the dinner hour – I know there is your father to care for, but I will have to leave you to sleep for several hours. I am hoping you will be able to continue without me."

"I suppose that remains to be seen. My father trained me as much as he was able. I've read all of the medical texts that he has."

He handed her an apron and tapes for her sleeves and then tied his own on.

"I'll give you my notes to review Friday night. You should get some idea of what I am testing for if you give them a thorough read. Also, you should take note of my method. It's not perfect, but I'm very exact in following the same process for each experiment."

"Do you not simply observe than?" she asked, donning the gear.

"I do. It will be easier if I go about my business as I normally would. I would like you to watch, and I'll explain what I'm doing as I do it. Does that sound reasonable?"

She nodded.

"Very well then. Shall we?"

****

"That is disgusting." Miss Isherwood held her breath, seemingly fascinated by the procedure. "I won't ever have to do it, will I?"

John gave her a half-smile.

"On me, or on you?" he asked, withdrawing the syringe from his arm. Beside him on the table stood several stoppered vials in a tray. Miss Isherwood had dutifully labeled them earlier that day after accompanying him to the local morgue where he had removed the blood samples from two different bodies who had died from unassociated diseases. The undertaker, amply paid to turn a blind eye to John's activities, had stayed to leer at Miss Isherwood. No doubt he had hoped to catch her swooning at the sight of the bodies, but to John's satisfaction, she had held up admirably, the only clue to any distress being a whitened face.

Now, they sat in the lab while John contributed his blood to the sets of vials.

"No," he continued, wrapping a bandage around his arm. "I will never expect you to provide your blood. Of course, should you ever like to volunteer to contribute to the experiments, I would welcome your participation, but I understand if you find it undesirable."

"How long will the blood be viable?" she asked. She took the vial from him with overly careful hands and attached the label along its side.

"Well, the bodies were fresh, so as far as having a reaction, assuming my blood won't simply infect the dead cells, the samples should last for several days."

"Then you are trying to infect your blood? Why?"

"If the vampire blood can be proven vulnerable to an organism, I am that much closer to discovering a cure, perhaps by isolating the vulnerability and reproducing it with a different substance." John rose and unrolled his sleeve. This would be his twenty-seventh time he had provided blood for an experiment. But explaining the procedure to her renewed his enthusiasm and despite his words, he warmed to the subject. "Thus far, the only things that produce any effects are distillations of silver and garlic. But the effects of the latter essentially turn the blood to powder which doesn't give me much hope for surviving an injection of either."

Miss Isherwood muffled a laugh with her hand.

"Have you tried Holy Water and a Crucifix as well?"

John chuckled and tied his apron on. He wouldn't tell her that was a myth.

"Do you have the notes from the morgue?" he asked instead. "If you could make a catalogue of their symptoms, later this evening I can make a comparison to others that I have in my records. You can use my office. Tomorrow morning we can attempt to discern what our patients were suffering from. I'll be up here for several hours."

"What will you be doing?" she asked, already headed for the door.

He pulled out some scouring brushes and old newspapers.

"I get to clean animal cages."

****

The sun had set half an hour ago. John rushed through his preparations. His face, shirt, and pants were darkened with coal dust, his cape exchanged for a dark brown duster, and his shoes for a pair of boots bought off a dock worker. To disguise his smell from heightened vampire senses, he rubbed Maxwell's velvet sleeping pillow over himself. If he was truly committed, he thought as he placed Maxwell back on the cushion in his cage, he would go visit the stables and borrow a used horse blanket. *But I'm not that dedicated, now am I*, he silently asked Maxwell. With a final tug at what passed for a black neck tie he strode down the stairs and out the door to begin his first foray in spying.

He moved at a fast clip toward the earl's residence. It was unlikely that his quarry had already left. The man was known for hosting lavish dinners late in the evening, though he wasn't popular among the ton. He didn't attend the usual round of balls and sorties which made the matrons sniff with displeasure.

John mentally reviewed his plans. He would wait across the street in the park. When the carriage was called for, he would attempt to hide in the boot. John stopped short. That was a stupid plan. The earl was a vampire. He would be able to hear his heartbeat from less than fifteen feet away.

He continued walking, dodging a watchman busy lighting a lamp on the street.

New plan. Wait in the park. Follow at a discreet distance. The horses wouldn't be pushed to anything faster than a trot while navigating the streets. He could probably keep up if he ran.

The distance was decreasing at a rapid pace, bringing him to Waite's address much faster than he was prepared to accept. He ran into the park and settled himself in the shadow of a tree that had an unrestricted view of the earl's townhouse. The night was quiet and full of smells, almost all of them animal. If he listened to closely, or took a deep breath through his nose, he would become overwhelmed with all the sensations. He focused on blocking them out and stared at the town house, steadfast.

John was nervous. He swallowed and glanced around. It was a stupid thing to feel like someone should notice his lurking when, in truth, were he leaning against a tree for any other reason than spying, he wouldn't feel so conspicuous.

The front door opened. John tensed, straining his eyes to see, but the interior revealed no light. It was a black void.

John waited. Was someone going out? What were they waiting for?

The door closed again.

A carriage pulled by matched blacks moved up the street and came to a stop in front of the door. He thought he saw movement, but it was too hard to tell if someone was returning or leaving. Why hadn't he thought to bring a pocket telescope?

A rustling from behind him sent fear racing through him. He turned sharply, but not fast enough. Pain exploded on the side of his skull. Spots danced before his eyes as he began to slip to the ground. A hand grabbed his shoulder to hold him up, while the other clamped itself around his mouth. His blinked, attempting to retain consciousness, but then blackness closed in as he realized he had discovered yet another vulnerability.

CHAPTER 5

John heard himself groan as he came awake. Darkness met his eyes, but the steady throb of a human heartbeat thrummed in his ears. A splitting pain on the right side of his head cut through the noise and confused him for a moment before the memories came flooding back. He attempted to rise, but a hand roughly pushed him back down onto the hard surface on which he lay. Several feet away a lantern flared to life, revealing a table top beneath him, and, standing to the side, an enormous muscular man with thick blonde hair pulled back in a queue. His eyes were pale blue, and cold as the arctic. The heavy brow drew down and the nostrils flared in response to John's perusal. His square jaw tightened, and he brought his hands into full view. At the sight of what he held, John gasped in fear and scuttled back along the tabletop.

"Who are you? Are you one of them?" the man demanded harshly, raising the stake in his left hand. His right clenched a heavy wooden mallet. But as apparent as the weapon was, his accent grabbed John's attention. The man was a Prussian, a political ally. The empire was known for soldiering that was both intense and unremitting when dedicated to a cause. That didn't bode well for John, given the man's suspicions.

"My name is Grissom. I am a bacteriologist, a doctor. Please, don't." John asked, stretching out his arms defensively, as if there was any hope of stopping the man should he determine on carrying out his threat.

"Why were you spying on Waite?"

John bit back a curse. Why hadn't he thought to suspect that the earl had eyes on his own house?

"I was - was looking for – a - a friend."

"You're lying." The man raised the stake and took a step toward him. All of three feet lay between him and John.

"No, no, wait! I'm unarmed. What do you want? Can I offer you a ransom?" John's eyes darted around the room, desperate to discover something that would serve as some form of defense or a weapon. The room was plain, small. A thin pallet beneath a shuttered window stood on one side of the room, a battered trunk at its foot from which the faint smell of silver and garlic hung like a cloud. A pitcher and wash basin sat on a table against another wall, sharing the space with a clay bottle – brandy by the smell of it – and a short, squat cup. Nothing indicating a permanent residence was visible. No paintings hung on the dirty, whitewashed walls. No writing desk. No wardrobe. He guessed the room was rented.

The man paused. His clothing was well-cut, but practical and worn.

"A ransom? I thought you were just a surgeon."

"Yes," John nodded. "Yes, I am. But I have a rich patron who won't want to lose his work. Besides, you aren't going to just stake me to death?"

"Tell me what you were doing watching the earl's house and I might let you live."

The demand was a strange one. If the Prussian was employed by the earl, there was no chance he would survive the encounter. Was the man promising him anything to get the information? He didn't want to reveal his purpose to one of Waite's men. And how did the man know, or suspect, he was a vampire?

"Time's up," the man growled. He covered another two steps before John rolled off the other side of the table, keeping it between them.

"Wait, I beg you. Answer me one thing. Why would you stake me to death? Please answer. It's important?"

The raised hands faltered before firming again in their attack stance.

"Because I don't dare take any risks."

"Risks of what?"

"That you are one of them."

So the earl guarded his home with human vampire hunters. Wise move, if he wanted to ensure his safety against vampiric competitors.

"But if I'm not," John responded, hoping to discover more information, "you would be committing murder, and I would die believing I died unjustly at the hand of a Bedlam escapee. If I am one of 'them,' shouldn't you question me more?"

The man's brow furrowed in puzzlement.

"Should I know who you're talking about? Who 'they' are?" John asked. "I have my reasons for being outside the earl's home, but if you are friends with the earl, I can hardly tell you what they are. Are you? Are you a friend of Lord Waite's?"

"No."

The stake and mallet lowered a fraction of an inch.

John sagged with relief. He wasn't out of the woods yet, but at least he wouldn't be dragged before the earl and drained dry. The man backed away and dropped the stake and mallet on the other table within easy reach of him.

"So, who are you? It had better be important considering the lengths I went to orchestrate the operation you so inauspiciously interrupted." He pointed to a chair on the other side of the table from him. "Sit."

"Only if you promise not to come at me with that stake," John said.

"So you are one of them."

John snorted.

"I hardly think dying by way of a stake through the chest is the preferred manner of quitting this life, no matter who one is."

The man nodded his head.

"Very well. I promise. For now."

It was a good sign that the man was willing to compromise on the point. John left the safety of his side of the one table and sat in the chair in front of the other table.

"I'll ask again. Are you one of them?" the man asked.

"If by 'one of them' you mean vampire, than yes, I am."

The man tensed. John responded in kind. Then his abductor relaxed.

"You wear spectacles. The moonlight glinting off the glass nearly gave us away."

"Who is us? Who are you?"

"Gerhardt Van Helsing."

"Vampire hunter?"

"Tinker. You can call me Gerhardt."

Tinker. John shook his head. It was an innocuous cover, but he could hardly press the man.

"What's your interest in the earl?" Gerhardt asked.

"I suspect he is doing something which puts England in jeopardy. More I will not say."

Gerhardt sat down opposite from him and settled his elbows on the table. He ran his hands over his hair in a gesture that relayed weariness and frustration. He reached over and grabbed the bottle of brandy and cup off the table with the wash basin. Curiosity got the best of John.

"What operation did I interrupt?"

Gerhardt paused in the middle of his pour and then resumed.

"If I was at liberty to reveal the information, I would. But I'm not."

Interesting. He had heard a similar line from Lord Waite. Perhaps they were both employed by the Crown. Or by different crowns that were playing political games he had managed to walk into the middle of.

"So what was your plan? You were going to skulk in the shadows? Follow him around on foot?" Gerhardt asked.

John flushed.

"Something like that."

"For a vampire, you seem...wanting."

"Yes, thank you for pointing that out. The lump on the side of my head agrees with you. I am attempting to discover why."

"To what purpose?" Gerhardt asked around a mouthful of brandy.

"Scientific interest isn't enough?" John shrugged. "I'm hoping to stumble upon a cure."

"A cure? You think it's a disease?"

"Yes, I do. What do you think it is?"

"I've never thought about it. " He paused to sip at his brandy. "I think I would call it a curse."

"And here I took you for an enlightened man."

"Oh, I'm enlightened." Gerhardt set the brandy down, stretched out his legs and linked his hands behind his head. "I know more and have seen more than I will ever care to see of vampires and their ilk."

"And killed more too, I suspect."

The big Prussian didn't answer.

"Why do you believe it is a disease?" Gerhardt asked instead.

"It acts like a contagion. Or a parasite. It has an incubation period, an infection period, and it more or less kills its victim."

"Does it? The vampires I've met seem very much alive."

"I didn't mean to imply that I understand all the aspects of the disease," John snapped. He settled his hands together in his lap. "Are you going to kill me?"

Gerhardt gave him a penetrating stare and then collapsed his hands onto the table.

"No. I think you're of more use to me alive."

"I won't be blackmailed."

"I wouldn't think so. Do you feed on humans?"

"No. Never. I keep a cow on some property just outside of Town."

Gerhardt gave a smile devoid of humor. "You surprise, Mr. Grissom. You might be the first honorable vampire I've met."

"Then you are unfortunate to have met so few. There are others."

"Yes, others – who live in secret, hiding their deformity from the eyes of the world."

John started to his feet.

"I refuse to sit and be insulted in such a manner. I was once a man, the same as any other."

"Going to call me out? Shall we duel at dawn?" Gerhardt drawled sarcastically, eyebrows raised. His light Prussian accent produced a strange mockery of the words. "Sit down, Mr. Grissom. Please. I apologize for my lack of compassion. In my experience, vampires are monsters who would drain me as soon as look at me."

John slowly sat back down.

"The enemy of my enemy is my friend." Gerhardt resumed. "If you would be so kind as to provide me some information as to the purpose of your night vigil, you might find, as I expect I will, that our stars align."

"You are a vigilante?"

"Are you? I am not. I cannot give you any details, but I would be very much surprised to learn that your information exceeds my own. Nevertheless, you could prove a useful ally."

"And in exchange?"

"You mean other than 'I won't kill you?'" Gerhardt paused for a beat and then continued. "I will relay to the proper authorities any information I think pertinent to your... mission."

"That would require my telling you what that is. And my trusting you enough to believe that you answer to the Crown."

"Yes."

John sighed. He couldn't see the harm in it. And he would like to receive another point of view on what he had learned. He began with the dinner and overheard conversation and ended by relaying the revelation of his closeted session with Mr. Isherwood.

"This Mr. Isherwood, is he a good man, a moral man?"

"As much, or more, as anyone I have yet met. I admit my acquaintance with him is not extensive, so I could be wrong. But he is at least sincere."

Gerhardt nodded. "I favor first impressions-"

"More's the pity."

"In your case, yes. But if you tell me you believe him to be a man of honor, I count that a good sign. I will want to meet him myself. Could you arrange that?"

"Pfft. I could hardly introduce you as my acquaintance, the tinker."

Gerhardt favored him with a look that shot ice water through John's veins.

"I'm sure I'll come up with something," he assured. "So what do you want me to do?"

"Go home. Work on a cure." He sighed heavily. "Your fumbling attempt to take things into your own hands will set me back at least a week, maybe two. I will have to reorganize everything. I might need you."

It didn't sit well with John to be told he was incompetent. He had tried in earnest, after all, and seemed to be receiving precious little credit for not just letting it go. But he didn't want to argue with a man who probably had an extensive collection of vampire trophies. John shivered involuntarily. Gerhardt might be human, but he was no ordinary human. Who kept a trunk full of vampire killing equipment in their traveling portmanteau?

In truth, no matter how Van Helsing insulted him, he would have to do what he could to ensure that Waite's intentions were discovered. When he had taken the

Hippocratic Oath, he had meant it – even if that meant putting himself at risk by not turning a blind eye to a conspiracy of murder and treason.

John took out his pocket watch. It was surprisingly early still. Only nine twenty. He must not have been unconscious long, which meant they were not excessively far removed from Waite's townhouse.

"You promise to let me know if you see anything untoward?" John asked, pausing in his stride toward the door.

"In as much as it applies to your quest, yes." Gerhard pulled out a small notebook and a nub of pencil from his pocket and tossed it onto the table. "Leave me your direction."

John hastily scribbled down the address to the lab. He itched to know what were Gerhardt's own concerns with Lord Waite, but he was hardly about to ask.

Moments later he was following the hallway down a set of narrow stairs to a door that led onto the street. Outside a waiting hackney silently accepted his directions and he set off. He gently probed the lump that lay on the side of his skull.

The brute had never apologized for thumping him so soundly.

The carriage moved through streets that intermittently collected the drunken and riotous. Untouched by the sight of the lower classes, young debutantes passed by accompanied by elderly matrons, their tittering, shrill laughter cutting through the clattering of their carriage wheels on cobblestones. One might think they felt the need to assure everyone they were indeed happy.

The laboratory's bow windows were dark and unwelcoming. Miss Isherwood had left for the night. He let himself out and paid the driver.

The carriage rumbled away and movement at the end of the street caught his attention. By the light of the lone lantern dimly illuminating the street on a corner, he could see the silhouettes of a man and woman struggling. His first instinct was to assume that the altercation was between man and wife, and to leave it. He wasn't about to insert himself into a lovers spat. Not normally, anyway.

He looked again. There was something eerily familiar about the young woman, who, with the use of a parasol, appeared to be winning the round. With a horrified gasp, he recognized the slight form of Miss Isherwood.

He jumped down off the steps and ran toward the pair at a sprint. Before he reached them, however, the man broke free and dashed off. Miss Isherwood stood with her back to John and jabbed her closed parasol in the air.

"And don't make the attempt again!" she shouted.

"Miss Isherwood!"

She jumped and gave out a short scream, holding her free hand to her chest.

"Good heavens, Mr. Grissom. I beg you will give a lady some warning in the future. You shouldn't slink up on one so."

"Slink?"

"It's a word," she defended under her breath and then said louder, "I was on my way home when that ruffian attempted to make off with my reticule."

John faced her dead on and made a careful study of her. Her heart rate still raced, and a faint tremor came and went in her fingers, most likely the after effects of her defense. At least all of her limbs seemed to be working like normal.

"You were fortunate. That encounter could have ended very differently. I apologize for not enquiring how you were going to return home. I assumed that you would hire a hackney. I will make arrangements with a local service."

"Truly, that's not necessary," she said, shaking the parasol. "It's no ordinary parasol. Leaded."

"Now, why does that not surprise me? Especially on a night like tonight."

She gaze up at him, mute, but curious.

"I beg you will humor me in this," John said instead. "I will be out often in the evenings. I would feel much more secure knowing I needn't fear for your safety."

She shook her head at him but smiled.

"If you insist."

"I very much do. Now, if you have no objections, I will walk you home."

Miss Isherwood took his arm.

****

John blinked his eyes and picked up his head. The sickly sweet smell of death and flowers was overpowering in his room. It was pitch black, but he could still sense a presence – vampire since he had detected a heartbeat only once in the five seconds since he had woken.

"Who's there?"

"Waite."

There was the sound of a match striking and the candle next to his bed flared to life. The earl held the yet lit match to the end of a cheroot.

"Please, smoke away in my bedchamber. I always take callers at… whatever time of night it is."

Waite puffed several more times, his basilisk-like black eyes probing John's. Finally, he reached inside his coat pocket and pulled out a small vial.

"The serum." Waite said. "Have you made your decision?"

No, he hadn't. But neither did he want to waste an opportunity to acquire more information. Infiltration it was.

"Yes."

"And?"

John took the cure from Waite's white gloved fingers. The blood was divided into two different components, a syrupy clear liquid and the darker, almost black, thick blood cells which had settled at the bottom of the vial.

"I need to isolate the compound in vampire blood which makes them immune to disease."

"Yes."

"Whose blood is it?"

"No one you know."

"But are they normal?" John swallowed back his humiliation. "Or are they like me?"

"Defective?" Waite arched a brow at him. "The blood comes from an excellent specimen. Made to order, as it were."

John fought the sneer of disgust that threatened to spread over his features. Waite had as good as admitted that he was turning people against their will. It was one thing for a man to volunteer himself as a slave to a vampire – he knew there were those sick enough to do it. But it was altogether another to create a personal army, even if of one, by turning them against their will.

He would bet his life that a cure was the last thing Waite hoped to procure. But what his end game was, he did not know. He needed more information. And Gerhardt or no, he wasn't about to sit around twiddling his thumbs.

John nodded. He would do it. Or at least he would study it and perhaps find what made them vulnerable to garlic and silver. It wasn't all that different from what he was already doing. The great difference was that this blood was normal vampire blood and he was looking to discover what it was about pure vampire blood that accounted for their increased speed and strength, seeming immunity to ill health and physical weakness, and heightened senses.

"Good." Waite took another puff of his cigar.

"Anything else, or are you going to stand watch over my bed all night?" John asked.

"I spoke with Francis Isherwood. I suspect you are aware of it, after hiring Miss Isherwood as an assistant. Her father was impressed with you."

"What did you want with him?"

"I offered him and his daughter a place to live. Free of the strictures of Town society."

"What, bury them in the country? He would never force his daughter to comply."

"Everyone has a price, dear Grissom."

"What was his?"

"More blood. His daughter doesn't realize he is starting to require more and more blood. No doubt due to his oddly ailing health." The earl's lip furled in disgust. "He, also, is defective. There are some advantages in his taking the arrangement. A blood slave among them."

"One of your minions?" John bit out.

Waite waved off the question with his cheroot.

"You are yet young. You have no vision of the world we can create."

John scaled back his venom. If he wanted Waite to hold him in confidence, arguing with him would hardly support the cause.

"And Miss Isherwood, is she in danger?"

"No, not from me. No vampire, or their relations, are."

As if that didn't beg the question about everyone else.

"Of course, unfortunate accidents do happen." Waited added. "At the worst time, too, such as when I am still recovering from some disappointment."

John would have to do something, find an alternative for Mr. Isherwood. If worse came to worse, he would demand they take up residence in his cottage and make free use of his cow. He would hate for the surgeon to fall back into habits he knew the man now despised. If only there was a way to preserve blood.

"Now, it's been a lovely chat, but another important engagement awaits." Waite ground out the end of the cheroot on the sill and tossed the remainder into the empty fireplace.

"Wait," John said.

The earl paused on his way to the window.

"What's your interest in the Isherwoods?"

Waite cocked his head as if he were about to say something, but then shrugged his massive shoulders.

"What's yours?" Waite asked.

The earl went out through the window with a silent whisper of silk. After a moment, John threw himself out of bed and watched as the man confidently took a path through the neglected back garden to the adjacent stables. From there, John knew, there was only one accessible street.

At best, John only had moments to decide. He could follow Gerhardt's injunction to leave the spying to more capable hands, or he could follow the earl himself.

He knew before the thought had even finished itself what he would choose. And it wasn't as if he had sought the earl out to follow him. John sprung from the bed and threw on a pair of pants over his night shirt. He stuffed his feet into a pair of boots, and hurriedly shrugged into a jacket as he sprinted down the stairs for the back entrance.

With infinite care to stay silent – he didn't want to come under the scrutiny of Waite's superior senses – he eased the door open and slipped out. The fetid sweet smell left a clear trail through the shrubs. John followed it as swiftly and silently as possible, and hoped he wouldn't come too close or find himself upwind.

He came to the back corner of the stable yard. It was still and quiet. He clung to the shadows against the building and peered around the side, hoping to find his quarry. His hopes did not go unrequited. Waite was just stepping into a waiting carriage. The driver set off at a near funereal pace which made following an easy feat, for now.

John didn't dare follow them too closely.

An hour later, they had gone from Mayfair to Marylebone to the outskirts of St. Giles. More than once, John had had to flee a boisterous drunken affair spilling its way out onto the street, or punch a would-be thief in the nose. He was relieved when the carriage came to a stop before entering the rookeries. He ventured to say even a lone vampire wouldn't stand a chance of residing there for any length of time.

John pressed himself up against the wooden façade of a building that named itself a theater, but which could barely seat more than a hundred people for its size. In the deep shadow of its overhang, on this moonlit night, he wouldn't be seen.

A short, thick-muscled man approached the carriage window. Moments passed. John squinted to see further into the dark, near moonless night. Something exchanged hands. Payment? Instructions? The carriage began to move again and the man stepped back, the object still in his fingers.

John left his hiding place and lurched into the street, imitating as best as he could remember, an intoxicated member of St. Giles.

He was but a few feet away when he realized the man was fully human. Was this another slave? Another conspirator? He needed a good look at the object. Whatever it was, it must be important for his lordship to drive all the way down here.

The man's back was to him as he walked down the street. John stumbled into his shoulder, knocking the item loose just enough for him to slip it from his fingers. And then he ran at a sprint in the opposite direction.

"Oi! Come back here!" The man was hot on his heels. John once again rued the fact that his own turning had been defective. The man's speed at least matched his own. The pounding footsteps were gaining on him, in fact.

Suddenly his feet flew out from under him. Hands, shoved him down and a fist connected first with one cheek and then with the other. A jab to his nose sent his head reeling back to connect with the cement. Pain bloomed along his jaw and he was sure, had he any blood to bleed, his nose would be a font of liquid. Without a full moon to lend light, the darkened visage above him, further shadowed beneath a rolled edge derby, was near invisible. John, feeling cornered, felt his canines surge to life, extending past his lower lips as he hissed in anger.

The man startled for a moment, just long enough for John to throw him off and begin his own attack. He made free use of every technique he had ever had the chance to learn in his stint at Gentleman Jack's. Bare knuckle fighting wasn't his preferred form of interaction, but if it was called for, he wasn't about to show himself in bad form.

He didn't think the man could kill him, but he might be susceptible to being laid low, and that would never do. John was able to get in a good punch on his jaw and then follow it up with a round kick to his chest. The man's momentum thrust him toward the street.

Each moment of his fall seemed to break and stretch as John saw the carriage that neither of them had noticed in the midst of their fighting. Bobbing lanterns hanging from either side of the carriage cast dancing shadows over their section of street.

The man fell, the horses' hooves came down, and then the front wheels rumbled over the body with a horrible disjointed lifting of the carriage, followed by the back wheels. The man's mangled remains, a dark shadow behind the carriage, lay in a distorted heap. Horror etched lines way across John's brow and on the sides of his mouth. The carriage slowed. The driver shouted.

With a jerk, John realized he couldn't be caught at the scene. If Waite knew who had absconded with his secrets, John wouldn't stand a chance. Had he been noticed? He didn't wait to find out.

John ran toward the nearest alley, a narrow divide between two buildings. It turned left. He ran through the maze of alleys and streets, listening closely for sounds of pursuit, but finding none. He finally paused and bent over, resting his hands on his thighs to catch his breath. Why he should be breathing hard when his heart and lungs had done so little to exert themselves, he did not know. Perhaps when he discovered more information about vampiric blood, he would know. His mind repelled against the memory of the man's body falling. Were he capable of nausea, he knew he would be tossing up his accounts right now. But he wasn't. All the pain was centered in his mind. He had no doubt the man was dead.

What if he was just a family man, blackmailed into doing Waite's bidding? What if he was a veteran, hard up for work, and had volunteered himself as an errand boy? His thoughts raced through scenario after scenario. He groaned and shook his head. If he continued on in this way, he would never get home. He would wallow in misery and offer himself up to the closest watch. And, if the conversation he had overheard at Waite's was anything to go by, he couldn't afford to do that. John shoved away all the hypotheticals he had begun casting up to himself. He straightened and patted his front coat pocket to make sure the cylinders were still in his possession.

His journey back was spent more than half the time with one eye cast over his shoulder. The route was full of twisting streets and buildings that branched out over the street. He would probably lose himself en route to the moderately better side of Town, but wouldn't he deserve it for stealing – borrowing, because he would return it – what he realized now was a series of bound scrolls? If he could discover more elements to Waite's conspiracy, he could better pinpoint how to stop it, or at least have evidence to present to the Prince Regent.

John had no clear idea what time it was by the time he came up on his street. From the sight of the milk cart going through, however, he guessed it was early morning. He was so aware of his prize, he was afraid it would somehow burn its way out of his pocket. He took it out as he ran up the steps to his house and let himself in.

Moments later he was sitting in his shuttered drawing room. A fire crackled in the hearth. A branch of candelabras burned brightly on the table next to him. He pulled at the black ribbon which bound all the scrolls together. It fell to the floor and he pulled out the first sheet and held it to the light. And then groaned in frustration. The scrolls – rolled up letters in actuality – were written in a cipher. Things couldn't just be easy now, could they?

CHAPTER 6

"What's his name?"

A stifled scream followed the question. John lifted his head from the microscope and looked toward the rear of the room. Miss Isherwood slapped her hands on her apron in frustration. It appeared one of the monkeys had favored her hand with a serving of his excrement.

"Van Helsing. He's Prussian." John said. It was a struggle to keep the smile off his face, but he managed.

"I think I just discovered a newfound hatred of monkeys."

"Which one is it?"

Miss Isherwood shut the cage door.

"Number 32."

"Ah, yes." John bent over his microscope again. "He's a nasty one."

"So, Mr. Van Helsing beat you over the head, kidnapped you, and then somehow got you to help him in his secret mission against Lord Waite?" She dunked her hands into a pot of water fresh-warmed from the stove, vigorously scrubbed with soap, and then doused her hands with a bottle of home brewed liquor.

"That about sums it up."

John blinked his eyes. The only good thing that might come out of what he was coming to call the 'Waite Episode' in his life would be the attainment of a new lens for his microscope. He could barely see the miniscule organisms free floating in the drop of serum he had placed on the glass.

"Miss Isherwood," John asked. "Would you be so kind as to redirect the light ever so slightly? Perhaps more light would help me see these cells well enough to draw them. I don't recall ever seeing anything quite like them before, but I could be wrong. I'll need to compare my notes."

"The morning is almost gone," she said, adjusting the turn screw on the mirror just enough to cast a sunbeam onto the highly polished metal plate above which the glass hovered on the microscope. "I don't know if it will help much. Is that better?"

John gave a noncommittal grunt. After several moments he shook his head. He could just make them out. The elongated ovals were covered in nodules and were noticeably smaller than red blood cells. He removed the glass, dumped it into the waiting alcohol bucket, and then went through his hand washing routine.

"I hate having to interrupt my work for my Monday morning feeding. It puts me back almost another day. It's not a complete loss, however. I believe I was able to see enough to sketch the components of the serum. After I do so, I have a project I think we should work on," John said. They both removed their aprons and went down the stairs to his office.

"Did you bring anything to eat?" John asked. He sat down at his desk and pulled out a pencil and sketch pad.

"Yes. Although, even with my hands thoroughly soaped and then drenched in your homemade alcohol, I'm still wary of eating with them. If I didn't have just one pair of kid gloves, I'd consider using them when I can." Miss Isherwood pulled a satchel out of her locker from which she unwrapped a napkin holding several rolls and a piece of cheese.

"That's an excellent idea, Miss Isherwood. I'm surprised I didn't think of it myself. But perhaps I wouldn't since I seem to be immune to disease."

"Well," she paused to swallow, "there's another vampire power you have then."

John drew the outer shape of the cell and then began adding the nodules at closely spaced intervals.

"Power?" he murmured. "Ah, yes. I suppose in my line of work, it is a distinct advantage. I hope you don't fall prey to any illnesses because of your exposure here."

"Perhaps if I'm lying at death's door, I'll allow you to turn me," Miss Isherwood chuckled.

John started. "Perish the thought!" He bent over the paper again. "I don't think I could anyway. I've only seen it happen once. It's a truly gruesome business that I have no desire to ever participate in."

The humor died from Miss Isherwood's eyes.

"I'm sorry. I suppose I shouldn't joke about it like that."

She continued eating, her brows drawn together in thought. John finished his drawing and lifted it up for her perusal.

"Fascinating," she said. "Does it move in that clear gelatin-like liquid?"

"No. There are an innumerable amount of them. They all lay flush against each other, although their nodules prevent them from lying in straight lines. Now," John set the drawing aside and pulled out the set of scrolls from a locked drawer. He tugged at the black ribbon and they fell open, curling up against each other. "This is the new project."

Miss Isherwood approached the other side of his desk. She pulled one out and held it toward the light.

"I don't understand. What is it? Is it a ciphered message?"

"Exactly so." John pulled one out from the stack. "I want to make sure we notate the order of them. I don't know if they are chronological, if they are instructions, or if they pertain to Gerhardt's or to my own mission."

"Gerhardt?" she asked, looking up from the scroll.

"Van Helsing."

"Right. Does he know about them then?"

John sawed his mouth back and forth. He didn't want to inform Gerhardt, but that was his pride talking. He didn't like the idea of Van Helsing taking over his investigation, even if he was more competent. The man was obviously a veteran of dealing in the shadows. And it wasn't as if John was an uncivilized brute who felt the need to assert dominance over his 'kill.'

It made more sense to reveal the coded scrolls to Gerhardt and then the three of them could work on decoding them together, assuming Gerhardt didn't pack them off and send them to Prussia or Whitehall.

"Not yet, but I think I have to tell him." John said.

"And you don't want to."

"What I want is to discover Waite's plans and stop them."

She lay the piece of vellum on the table.

"A noble cause, but wouldn't it be easier to infiltrate? Pretend Lord Waite is a friend? You could attend some of his vampire events, go to his dinners? He might welcome your friendship."

John shook his head.

"You are not in a position to know, but this is a man who crosses lines I refuse to even approach. I won't be put in the position of being tempted to take of another human being."

"You never have then? What about when you first turned?"

"That is a story for another day." Possibly never, since it was a memory he didn't care to revisit any time soon.

"I beg pardon for prying." She gave him a rueful smile and began packing up her lunch. "I am so used to my father. He is almost flippant about being a vampire. Just with me, of course, but I have so little exposure other than him."

Because she wouldn't know the difference unless they told her, he realized.

"Maybe we should have some sort of a secret signal for those moments when someone is a vampire. At least then you will know to be careful," John said.

Miss Isherwood paused. "No, I don't think I would like that. I don't want to become a person who is suspicious of his own shadow. And while there are many bad vampires, not all are without honor – one need only see yourself – and there are normal men who are just as evil."

John shrugged. He might have a preference, but he wouldn't insist.

She came back to the desk.

"Are you going to get some rest this afternoon? I recall your saying that you would need to from here on out," she said.

"No. Not today. Possibly never. Gerhardt has assured me my skills are not only unnecessary, they might prove detrimental to the cause."

A sour look crossed Miss Isherwood's features.

"I don't like him already. How can you be that bad? Even children know how to sneak cookies."

"Hmm… this would be more like sneaking milk from a cat."

Her eyebrows shot up.

"Anyway," he continued, "I am sufficiently rested. After Mass yesterday, I slept like the dead – no pun intended – woke to shine my boots, iron my shirt, brush my coat, and then promptly returned to my bed. I will work on cataloguing these letters, transcribing the symbols into a table."

"And me?"

John rose from his desk and pulled opened a locked cabinet that stood along one wall.

"I want you to see if you find any drawings resembling that sketch." He pulled out three wooden crates and stacked them on the floor. "Here are my journals. The first few are in the top box. They aren't as thorough, but they were when I was yet young. I didn't have a method yet. It'll be tedious work, but between my journals, the medico journals," John waved toward a full bookshelf, "and the medical treatises," he waved toward another full bookshelf, "you quite possibly could remain busy for the next two months."

86

Her shoulders drooped.

"Joy," she said.

"I know. Being a research assistant is not all diverting amusements, and flung poo, but if you find yourself overcome by tedium, feel free to take a walk, visit the monkeys, or alphabetize my bookshelf." John grinned. "I'll have a desk delivered for you tomorrow. In the meantime, you may use mine."

"Where will you work?"

"I will work in the sitting room. I should mention, too, that I don't have tea on hand, but should you want some I can bring in the supplies tomorrow. A friend in the Medico Society gave me an excellent mix recently, but unfortunately, I don't have much of a taste for it."

"That would be heavenly." She dropped her gaze to her laced fingers. "Thank you for offering that. My father and I can't afford to…. Well, let's just say, I'll be happy to keep my tea canisters at home."

John pursed his lips. He really couldn't enquire as to how straightened their circumstances truly were, but he was starting to think her accepting this position was a move borne of desperation. He only hoped she would tell him if the pay wasn't enough. He was tempted to broach the topic of her father's increased appetite, but how could he propose their occupying his cottage? She was a woman of virtue, she might be offended he would even suggest it.

He realized she was now looking at him, expecting him to respond. The tips of his ears began to burn.

"It's my pleasure. I hope you will –" John interrupted himself, and then smiled. "Happy hunting, Miss Isherwood."

He left the room, scrolls in hand. What must she think of him?

****

Tuesday morning. The light was beginning to fully flood into his window. Part of him wanted to jump up out of bed and rush down to the laboratory, but an equally strong part of him pulled him back toward the comfort of his pillow. He had fallen asleep somewhere around three in the morning. The code had been broken down into its various characters, but every attempt to discover the key had been a failure. He tried to motivate himself to rise by calling to mind all the various aspects of his project that needed the morning light for progress, but his mind wasn't even capable of such thoughts. He slid back into sleep without noticing.

John started. A beam of sunshine was shooting through a crack in his curtains and slicing across his eye. What time was it? The ormolu clock on the mantel said ten in the morning.

He groaned and rolled off the bed. His personal toilette would have to make some concessions to his time constraints. How could he have spent a whole three hours of the morning's light sleeping? Even if he could grant that the human mind worked more efficiently when well rested, it also remained true that bright morning sunlight was a requirement for the advancement of his work.

A half hour later, he was running up the steps to the front door of his laboratory, a canister of tea beneath one arm. He let himself in and – stopped. The muted sound of voices reached his ears as well as an unfamiliar waft of a human scent he had smelled before, but couldn't place. His head craned to hear better, but the words, carrying down the stairs from the upper drawing room, were not distinguishable.

It was odd of Miss Isherwood to entertain at his laboratory, but at least she would have tea and a cracked set of ceramic ware to serve it in. He took the stairs two at a time and slowed before he was visible from the open drawing room door. It wouldn't do to have her think there was some emergency. Shared laughter met his ears as his head came abreast the top of the stairs.

"Ah, Mr. Grissom. Welcome to the party." Miss Isherwood rose to her feet as his own reached the landing. Her guest was yet hidden in the room, but when he stepped inside, he wasn't surprised to see a massive blonde figure taking up a divan. He rose upon John's entrance, but slowly.

"Herr Doktor." Gerhardt's heels snapped together and he gave a short, clipped bow.

"Herr Van Helsing."

Miss Isherwood glanced back and forth between the two men.

"We were both expecting you here earlier, Mr. Grissom. I hope you don't mind my having let him in?"

"Not at all. You might work here, Miss Isherwood, but I'm not in a position to be making decisions on whom you will receive."

John didn't like the fact that Gerhardt had won past Miss Isherwood's natural reserve so quickly. Next thing they knew it would be walks in the park and rides down to Hatchard's. He realized that he was being unreasonable, but for reasons he didn't care to contemplate too deeply, he felt the smiles she favored the tall Prussian with were entirely too friendly.

"I assume you have some news for me?" John asked.

"No, I was hoping you could make the time for an introduction to Mr. Isherwood."

"My father?" Miss Isherwood exclaimed. John hadn't told her yet of Gerhardt's interest. "Why do you wish to meet him?"

"I find his association with Lord Waite puzzling. But Grissom tells me he's trustworthy. I need to decide that for myself."

"And if he's not? Are you going to stake an old, ailing man?" Miss Isherwood's words were combative but her tone was sarcastic.

"Not when they have beautiful, intelligent daughters to provide for."

Miss Isherwood snorted inelegantly. John rolled his eyes.

"This beautiful, intelligent daughter might be able to provide for herself soon. I will, of course, take exception to any intimation that my father is less than an honorable man."

"To umbrage, then," Gerhardt said, tipping a chipped cup in her direction.

"Ah, yes, Miss Isherwood, I brought you the tea." John held out the tin in her direction and received the satisfaction of having her cradle it in her arms with a happy smile. She opened the tin and took a deep whiff. She closed her eyes.

"Mmmm… it's much too splendid to use for everyday tea time, but since we have a visitor, and you don't take tea, I'll make us a small pot."

"Excellent." Miss Isherwood left the room and John clasped him hands behind his back. The man had invaded his space. Within all of ten minutes, he had wormed his way into a tea time. He had pushed John out of his own investigation. If the strain of his coat against his biceps were any indication, he had muscles on top of his muscles. His firm straight jaw, plus the added benefit of his height, would probably have any young woman swooning. It really was too much. Why hadn't he thought to pay closer attention to Miss Isherwood's heart beat? It would have been a good indicator of just how much Gerhardt was affecting her.

"Were you going to tell me?" Van Helsing asked.

"Tell you about what?" It wasn't as if he didn't know, but he wasn't about to give Gerhardt the satisfaction.

"The coded scrolls."

90

"Did Miss Isherwood tell you about them?" The question came out sharper and more like a growl of anger, than John intended.

"No."

"Then how-?"

"I may have been watching your house last night."

"You weren't. I would have noticed."

"I haven't survived this long without knowing how to get around vampires."

John shook his head. He didn't believe him. Gerhardt pulled a thin, small journal from one of his pockets and flipped it open.

"9:00 pm, Library: read a book for ten minutes. 9:10 wandered around the house. 9:20 returned to Library, pared candles. 9: 30 sat down at desk and pulled out scroll. 9:43 tossed scroll across the room. 9:45 retrieved scroll, resumed assigning characters to letters without success –"

"That's quite enough. I think you've made your point." John was seething. Just the thought of anyone watching him, much less a vicious vampire-hunter, made his throat constrict like his cravat had been tightened too much. "Why?"

"I had to make sure my initial impression of you wasn't wrong. One can never be too careful."

"And? Your conclusion?"

The rattle of china on china announced Miss Isherwood's return only seconds before she entered the room.

"Morning, gents. Hope you were having a lovely coze," she said, setting the tray down on the table.

John stiffened. She was mistaken if she assumed he and Van Helsing were friends.

CHAPTER 7

"I just want you to know, I fail to see the point of this," John said. The three of them stood in a staggered line on the steps of the Isherwoods' modest rooms. "He is an old man. Hardly a threat. And I don't know why you agreed to it, Miss Isherwood."

"Is he always so surly in the morning?" Gerhardt asked cheerfully.

Miss Isherwood chuckled as she opened the door.

"I'm not such pleasant company in the morning myself, so we generally avoid each other for a good two hours after I arrive at the laboratory."

They followed her inside, but came to a stop at the unearthly howl that met their ears from the chambers above them. Miss Isherwood's face whitened. John eased in front of her, bringing all his senses to the fore to determine the threat. A tang of desperate hunger filled the air. It was a peculiar smell.

The odor, only perceptible to his vampiric senses, filled him with apprehension, as did the low-toned thumps and groans that continued to sound in the upper floors.

"Miss Isherwood, has your father fed today?" John whispered. He kept his voice calm, but tension wrapped around his words. Van Helsing unbuttoned his coat, revealing a motley assortment of gear strapped to a belt around his waist. He unscrewed two different flasks on his hip and moments later John's eyes widened and he jerked back, his blood repelled by the odor of garlic.

"What?" Gerhardt asked. "I never go out without taking precautions."

"I don't understand," Miss Isherwood. "I left him with three pints of beef blood, fresh from the butchers, this morning."

Gerhardt snorted.

"If he's not getting fresh from the source, it's no wonder his health is failing."

Miss Isherwood clutched her elbows against her side.

"Is he – do you think he's...." she trailed off.

"Dangerous?" John put in. "Yes. Yes, I do. I want you to go down to the butchers and get a gallon of blood, Miss Isherwood. Gerhardt, if you are up to the task, we will need to restrain him in some way."

Gerhardt went into an adjacent room and returned with a length of cord from the bell pull. John moved toward the stairs.

"You're not going to – to kill him, are you?" Miss Isherwood asked reaching out her hand.

"No." John looked over at his tense companion. "We're not."

"Unless we have to," Gerhardt muttered. "My going up there will be like putting a steak in front of a starving man. Only much worse."

"We won't have to," John said. He squeezed Miss Isherwood's fingers and continued up the stairs toward the source of the noise.

Two flights up and the stairs ended on a darkened landing. His senses prickled with awareness. Somewhere in the shadowy darkness, a vampire was writhing in pain. If he had to guess from the sounds alone, he would say they were fortunate Isherwood was not so far gone that he had left the house and attacked the closest person on the street.

He moved forward into the shadows, the only light in the long hallway streamed through pinpoint cracks in a shuttered window at one end of the hall. An attic was normally where the servant's quarters were, but since the Isherwoods didn't have servants, it made sense that the layers of dust showed only a single set of footprints.

John pointed to a closed door through which issued bestial groans, panting, and the telltale clacking of a vampire close to the edge of losing his sanity. John winced, his mind's eye seeing Mr. Isherwood's jaws involuntarily snapping together. Whether Miss Isherwood liked it or not, her father would have to be moved into John's cottage for his, and her, own safety. And he would have to redouble his efforts in discovering a cure.

John reached out a hand, unsure if he should knock or just surprise the man, assuming he could be surprised. While Mr. Isherwood also suffered vampiric deficiencies, John had no idea whether or not the doctor's advanced state of hunger increased what vampiric abilities he had.

He opted for surprise and tried the door. Locked.

Looking over his shoulder at the six foot Van Helsing behind him, he made a kicking motion and held up three fingers. It was possible Isherwood was already aware of their presence, especially given Gerhardt's non-vampire heartbeat, but they would have to risk it.

In a weird moment of realizing things at unlikely times, John realized, as he stood aside and counted down to three, that he could barely hear Van Helsing's heartbeat, and he was standing right next to the man.

Both of their feet planted against the door in a swift, violent move. The lock broke off and the door splintered open.

Gerhardt stepped back and allowed John to go first – which made sense, since John was the vampire and Gerhardt wasn't. John reached out with his senses into the black, windowless room. He felt, more than saw, movement to his right. He had barely time to raise his arms before he was attacked and carried to the floor. He landed on his back, his spectacles flying off his face. Fingers clamped around his throat. John's hands sought purchase in folds of material. A jingling sound met his ears. Metal on metal. A chain?

The weight began to lift off him.

"Hold him down!" Gerhardt shouted. John grabbed what he could of Isherwood and pulled. A growl and howl resounded as the weight of the older man fell on him again. Suddenly, clawed fingers gripped him and a piercing pain shot through his left shoulder.

"He's biting me! Make haste, Gerhardt!"

John could feel his strength draining away from him as the vampire pulled great quaffs of blood out of him.

Light fell into the room. Through the collection of limbs he could see the silhouette of a woman in the doorway, a bucket in her hand.

"Miss Isherwood. Get out," he tried to shout, but weakness had begun to take his limbs and all he could do was watch as events unfolded. Gerhardt stood above them both, holding the cord in one hand and a flask in the other. The rope had been knotted in the middle multiple times until the knot resembled a small ball.

Gerhardt dumped the contents of the flask on Isherwood's fingers and head and tossed it aside. The liquid trickled onto John's neck, burning a trail to the floor. The smell of garlic seared John's nostrils, but it did the trick. The vampire's head reared up. He attempted to rise, but Gerhardt put a knee in his back and slipped the rope over his head and the large knot betwixt the gaping, bloodied jaws. He tied it behind Isherwood's head, effectively muzzling the rabid vampire.

In a remote way, as if his mind was disjointed from his body, John felt the increased pressure of both men on his abdomen.

Gerhardt was almost thrown off as Mr. Isherwood bucked and began clawing at the rope. Gerhardt grunted with effort and caught the man's hands, pinioning them behind his back and securing them with another piece of the cord.

The pressure on John's chest subsided as Gerhardt pulled Mr. Isherwood off of him. A haze began to creep in on the outside of John's vision, blocking out Isherwood's activity. The scent of the fresh beef blood wafted toward him, but the rapid thumping of Miss Isherwood's heart was the greater attraction. Despite the side of him that threw itself away from the thought of harming her, he began salivating, his fangs creeping down to edge over the sides of his lower lip.

He struggled against the temptation, turning away from the sight of her.

"Gerhardt!" His voice came out a throaty, ragged whisper. Isherwood had taken a lot from him.

The smell of the beef blood came nearer. A hand gripped his shoulder.

"Drink," Gerhardt said, and set the bucket next to him. John hauled himself up. He picked up the metal bucket with heavy hands and began pouring the thick liquid down his throat. Nothing else registered as his depleted stores were filled again. It was a cheap and disgusting fix, but it still created an exquisite pain. Finally, when his body could handle no more, he felt the bucket, now half-full, begin to slip from his fingers. Gerhardt caught it.

John collapsed back onto the dusty floor. He lay partially aware of his surroundings, but incapable of moving. Miss Isherwood still stood in the doorway, a hand clenched at her breast, ready to flee. Across from him, her father lay curled in a ball on the floor, his feet and legs bound, the rope bit between his fanged teeth.

Muted, meaningless words fell on John's ears, until, ever so slowly, they began to filter through to his consciousness.

"...neither of us expected it," Gerhardt said. "Do you have somewhere your father can stay?"

Miss Isherwood's distraught gaze flew from her father's figure to Gerhardt.

"No."

John tried to lift his head.

96

"I do," he tried to say, but his mouth was sticky with blood and it came out as an indiscernible croak of noise. Gerhardt whipped around toward him, the flask of silver water in hand. John wiped his mouth and chin on the arm of his ruined coat.

"They can stay at my cottage, near Fowlton," John got out, when he was sure most of the blood was gone.

Gerhardt handed him a handkerchief. "You missed a spot," he said, pointing to John's cheek.

"We'll need to get him fed before we go," John resumed, indicating Isherwood. "But we should go tonight."

He rose to his feet, swayed for several seconds, and then found his balance.

"Do you have your wits about you?" Gerhardt asked, holding out a cautionary hand.

John hated seeming vulnerable, but after his episode only moments before, it was understandable Gerhardt would be wary.

"I am not altogether back to my normal self, but I won't attack you, if that is what concerns you."

Miss Isherwood's hand unclenched. She reached down and picked up the lantern from the floor.

"Please help me get my father more comfortable, Mr. Van Helsing. I understand that he must remain bound, but I don't want him to be in pain. And I would like to feed him immediately, if I can. I have a tube downstairs I can use to pipe the blood into his mouth."

Gerhardt took Isherwood's shoulders while John took his feet. Despite his shoulder, weakened from the attack, they were able to get the man onto a bed in a neighboring room Miss Isherwood had cleared of dust coverings.

"Do sit down, Mr. Grissom, you are not looking at all the thing," she said. "After my father is fed, I should like to stitch up that wound on your shoulder. You're sure to end up with a gruesome scar if I don't."

"I pray you don't concern yourself, Miss Isherwood. It will heal well enough without stitches."

And so it would. But a garish ripping of flesh *was* sure to leave a scar without the stitches. He just didn't like the idea of his own assistant practicing her surgery on him. And, stupid as it was, his own ego demanded he pretend nonchalance.

"Don't be foolish. You won't be the first nor last patient I've stitched up. Of course, if you haven't the stomach for it-"

"You are being absurd. Do as you like," John said. And then immediately felt like a cur for being offended when he should have just accepted her offer in the first place. He shook his head. "My apologies, Miss Isherwood. Please forgive me. It's been a trying day."

She nodded.

"Apology accepted," she said and turned toward the door. She paused and said over her shoulder, "No guarantees that I'll be gentle, though."

John groaned.

"Hurry back," Gerhardt prompted. "Your father might break his bonds and that would be disastrous."

She disappeared around the corner, leaving Gerhardt to watch with him.

"Can you arrange for him to be moved tonight?" John asked.

"Yes. I don't like that we haven't been able to speak to him, but perhaps tomorrow he will be lucid enough to question."

"Question? Is he suspected of a crime?"

"No. But I want to know what Lord Waite visited him about."

Gerhardt rose to his feet and patted at his belt. After retrieving his flasks from the other room, he stopped at the door.

"I'm off to find a hackney. The sooner we get him settled, the sooner I can find my bed. I do need my rest."

"I imagine so, what with staying up all night watching my rooms," John said dryly.

Gerhardt left and moments later Miss Isherwood returned, ligature case in one hand and tubing in the other. She set the bucket on a table next to the bed and worked to prop her father up. He struggled and twitched his head at her, straining against the cord that held his wrists.

"Father, can you hear me?"

His red hazed eyes burned with manic intensity.

"You need to eat. I've brought you some blood."

She placed one end of the tube in the bucket, and put the other end to her mouth as if she was prepared to suck in a mouthful of blood.

"Stop," John said, jumping to his feet. "Allow me. Please."

She handed him the tube, a sigh of relief leaving her. John sucked blood through the tube and then quickly inserted it between the fangs and over the gag, pointing it toward the back of Isherwood's throat. He was trying to be careful but still managed to make a bloody mess everywhere. John glanced down at his own ruined clothes. By the look of them, Mr. Isherwood wasn't the only one in need of a change. Mr. Isherwood began to gulp and John raised the bucket higher to ensure the impromptu pump would maintain a constant flow.

"I suppose I should have dressed for dinner," John said into the quiet. Miss Isherwood barked a laugh and then dropped her face into her hands. He smiled at her. She tried to stifle her laughter, her shoulders shaking. Finally she gave up and peals of laughter turned into a hysterical release of tension that only ended after tears began wetting the corners of her eyes.

"Oh, goodness, that was idiotic," she said, when she could breathe again. "Thank you."

The faint ringing sounds of horses' hooves announced the return of their companion.

"Gerhardt has returned with our transportation," John said. Slurping sounds came from the bottom of the bucket. He removed the tube from Mr. Isherwood's mouth. The older man lay slumped against the bed pillows, his body slightly off to the side. His eyes were half-shut and his fangs almost fully receded. The peculiar smell of his desperate hunger was also gone. "The restraints may not be necessary in several moments."

Miss Isherwood rose to her feet and opened the ligature case.

"Sit. And pull your shirt off your shoulder." Having put on her surgeon mode, she was all brisk business. Despite her lack of guarantee to be gentle, she was careful not to cause him undue distress. In short order, with a minimum of reaction on his part, she had the ugly wound stitched up. His shirt was heavily spotted with blood, two jagged edged holes in both shirt and coat a testimony to the ordeal he had suffered. She thumbed the holes on his coat before handing it to him.

"I'm sure my father will make his own apologies when he comes to, but I am truly sorry for all this. At the same time, if you had not been here…." She looked down at her hands and then back at him, her eyes speaking all her fears. "I didn't realize his condition had degenerated so much as to require this much blood this often."

John shrugged into his coat, gingerly moving his left arm to do so.

"My cottage will be perfect for him. I will add another cow to my stock to ensure he has a ready supply."

"We can't repay you for that kindness. Not monetarily, anyhow. You will not do anything that endangers your living, I hope."

"Think nothing of it, Miss Isherwood. It does not affect my circumstances hardly at all. If my situation seems simple and plain, it is only because I am conservative by nature. I assure it will not affect my finances to any great degree."

A muffled sound interrupted them. Mr. Isherwood attempted to sit up from his position on the bed. Miss Isherwood rushed to his side. She sat on the bed and combed the white hair off his brow.

"Father?" She held his face in her hands, carefully studying his eyes. After a moment's perusal she reached behind him and untied the cord gag. He swallowed and worked his jaw, his gaze flitting about the room.

"Did I hurt someone?" he whispered.

"Nothing I can't recover from," John assured him. Mr. Isherwood's glance flew from his daughter to John.

A knock sounded on the doorframe. Mr. Isherwood looked up to see the tall figure of Van Helsing at the door.

"Father, may I present a new acquaintance. Gerhardt Van Helsing," Miss Isherwood said.

Gerhardt stepped forward and bowed his head.

"Van Helsing, the vampire hunter? In my house?!" Mr. Isherwood cried, even as his fangs fully extended and he tensed, prepared to attack. Though how he would manage with both legs and feet bound was anyone's guess.

"I see my reputation precedes me. I may be a vampire hunter, but you'll notice, I didn't kill you. Despite multiple opportunities to do so. I had to be convinced you would not prove a threat to my operations."

"And am I?"

"I was right to be cautious. Your daughter underestimated your needs."

"She wasn't to blame," Mr. Isherwood growled.

"No, you are," John said with severity. "You have an obligation to make sure your appetites are taken care of. What if we had not decided to stop by so unexpectedly? You would not have made it another two hours before losing your head and attacking someone in the street – and if you had lasted long enough for Miss Isherwood to return home, what sort of reception would she have had?"

It was not only the thought of what Miss Isherwood could have been subjected to that made him burn with anger, but also that because of Mr. Isherwood's foolishness, Miss Isherwood had seen him lose almost total control of himself, something he had never yet done and hoped never to do. "I expected more from you, sir."

Miss Isherwood stepped between them. "That's enough, Mr. Grissom. You forget yourself, sir."

John gave her father a pointed stare. "Do I?"

Isherwood hung his head at the rebuke.

"Unbind him," John said to Gerhardt. "The horses are standing and we haven't much time. Miss Isherwood, if you would be so kind as to acquire a small valise of clothes for your father, we will meet you in the carriage."

"What about my daughter? Have we no time to pack?" Mr. Isherwood poked his head around Gerhardt's head and shoulders.

"No, we must hurry if we are to ensure you have a constant blood supply come morning," John said.

"Don't worry, father. I'll accompany you there, but I will return here and continue to work as an assistant for Mr. Grissom."

"Unaccompanied? Unprotected?"

"Pish, posh, father. I am no debutante whose reputation is in need of protection. We are all but one rung above those who seek us out for treatment. And I won't stand on ceremony when Mr. Grissom is the only one who is working to discover the secrets behind vampirism. If he can find a cure –"

"Miss Isherwood. As much as I appreciate your arguments in my favor, time is of the essence. We must go," John said.

"Of course." She bent over her father and kissed him gently on his cheek. "I'll join you in a few moments."

She left them and Gerhardt and John began the struggle of getting the older man down the stairs. Fifteen minutes later she was stepping out of the house, a heavy valise in one hand, a cane and her parasol in the other. John took the items from her and placed them in the boot.

"I hate to think father will be without his books," Miss Isherwood said, before taking his outstretched hand and navigating the carriage steps.

"I visit the cottage regularly, at least three times a week," John said as they settled back against the squabs. "You are welcome to join me if you would like to bring books from your library or would just like to visit. I have no riding horses at the cottage but walking provides some attractive vistas," He continued on a different tack. "I hope you will not mind my stopping by my own house. I require a change of clothes."

"Is the cottage far?" she asked.

"Just outside of Town. It will seem more rusticated than it is. A half hour by carriage. I normally walk the last bit of it, but we are hardly fit to be seen and I don't want to tax your strength, Mr. Isherwood," John said, turning that gentleman.

"So, I finally meet another vampire who seems to suffer from unusual disabilities," Mr. Isherwood returned. "You wear spectacles. You are no more swift or strong than the average man with a natural athletic bent. Anything else?"

John felt his temperature rise and his glance skewed over to their other companion

, who smirked and tilted his hat forward to cover his face.

"It appears I can also be knocked unconscious."

Mr. Isherwood was dumbfounded.

"What kind of a vampire are you?!"

103

CHAPTER 8

The carriage rattled on into the night, the interior now and again flooded with candlelight from street lamps. Out of the corner of his eye he could see Miss Isherwood chewing back a smile, at his expense no less.

"Defective, obviously," John said, his tone dampening.

"I always assumed I never turned properly because I was an old man when I was attacked, but seeing you, I am inclined to believe there is something about our blood that refused it," Mr. Isherwood said.

"It's my belief the disease did not take fully," John said. "I suspect it is the same with you, which is why we can both withstand sunlight. Unlike you, however, my blood is able to repel any and all organisms it has been exposed to. Only silver and garlic have the usual disastrous effects. On the other hand, there must be a reason why, and I hope to discover that reason. And thereby discover a cure."

"A cure for vampirism?" Mr. Isherwood nodded slowly. "It never occurred to me to think of it in those terms. But it makes sense. Have you been testing on your own blood then?"

John nodded.

"You must take a vial of my blood as well. Broaden your comparison."

"Next time I am out at the cottage, I will bring my blood letting equipment. For now, I only wish to see you safely settled."

John looked over at Miss Isherwood, next to him on the carriage bench. She had leaned her head against the carriage's side, and, no doubt exhausted by the morning's events, had fallen asleep.

"I've a mind to have a discussion with you before we reach our destination, Mr. Grissom." The old man sat forward. Gerhardt appeared to be snoring beneath his hat. "My daughter tells me you are employing her as a laboratory assistant. I believe you are an honorable man, and my daughter is a capable woman. But if ever I should discover anything untoward is taking place…. You may be sure I will exact due recompense."

John's eyebrows shot up and he dropped his head. It didn't take much to suspect what Mr. Isherwood was warning him away from.

"Allow me to assure you, Mr. Isherwood, I am, and remain, a practicing Catholic." John dropped his voice. "If ever I have intentions towards your daughter, I will request your permission to court her. Nevertheless, I would be the basest scoundrel to pursue a courtship with one in my employ. Not to mention the fact that I am currently suffering an affliction which must necessarily preclude me from the married state. I trust that we understand each other?"

The carriage came to a stop at John's rooms before Mr. Isherwood made a response, but when the doctor relaxed back in his seat, John knew he believed him.

***

The cow, her tan hide seeming gray in the moonlight, lowed at him from over the fence, probably surprised to see him at an unaccustomed hour. They had arrived at the cottage in the early morning.

"Mr. Isherwood, I should like to acquaint you with Betsy. She is a prime blooder." John patted the side of her neck and offered a handful of grass.

Mr. Isherwood arched an enquiring brow.

"My own term. We refer to milk cows as milkers. I thought I would…." John trailed off at the sight of their unamused faces. "Right. Well, shall we see your new quarters, Mr. Isherwood?"

He ushered them into the modest home. The signs of recent use could be seen throughout.

"Betsy's keeper is a Scots vampire. He lives in the basement and comes out at night to work and clean and eat. I'll have him prepare a room for you. It is a simple life, but he seems to enjoy being a recluse. Once you are more settled, I imagine your different schedules will suit."

As he spoke, John walked them through the house, a lit candelabra held high in his hand. A small hall and oversize stone hearth dominated the interior. Whitewashed cupboards were neatly set up with plate ware. The upstairs bedrooms had yet to be aired, or dustcovers removed, but it was a welcoming, snug place. The trickle of spring water rushing through the cooling tank lent a merry, refreshing backdrop for their reception.

"Will you be comfortable here, do you think?" John asked.

Mr. Isherwood pegged the sleepy-eyed Gerhardt with an eye.

"As long as Mr. Van Helsing will consent to leave us alone, I shall be perfectly content," Isherwood said, before turning to his daughter. "Come then, girl, let's go explore our new quarters. If there are enough rooms, I should like to establish a correspondence area. Failing that, I may be obliged to take command of a desk."

Miss Isherwood mutely fell in behind him, taking but a moment to favor John with a look of happy surprise. He too, had not thought Mr. Isherwood would take to his new environment with such verve.

"I still need to ask him about his session with Lord Waite," Gerhardt said. "But it will have to wait until tomorrow. If you like, you may drop me off at the inn we passed. Also, you might purchase some items from the grocer for them. I noticed the larder was bare of all but a clean bucket."

John nodded. "I don't believe I can accomplish much more in the way of work for the day. The grocer should be open in several hours. We should take the opportunity to spread the word to the locals that her father is a pensioner of mine, so they won't be alarmed should they come across one or the other of them in the vicinity of the cottage."

It was taking an unexpected amount planning and time – more than he had thought requisite to get them settled. But having done so, it would be one less item of concern to him.

****

"I can hardly believe it is early afternoon," John slapped the reins in a futile effort to hurry the pony along. The sky had darkened and swollen clouds promised to unleash a torrent on the occupants of the now empty cart. "Who would have thought a trip to the grocers would be so time consuming."

"At least they will be set for the next month. I think you overdid it on the supplies," Gerhardt said. John turned around to look behind him, but Gerhardt sat on the back of the cart, his legs hanging off the edge and his back to John. Determining if the man was trying to be humorous was an exercise in futility.

"Maybe."

The first fat drops of rain began to fall out of the dark, swollen clouds above them. Within moments it was coming down in sheets, snaking its way down the back of John's collar. He was, for once, regretting not having brought his beaver.

They reached the inn ten minutes later. A boy tripped down the steps to the cart and waited for his tip in small coins. Gerhardt, his boots almost half-buried in mud, stared the boy down instead, but John dug into his waistcoat and found several pence. He followed the vampire hunter into the inn, the Flying Pheasant.

It had been over a year since inclement weather had forced him to seek shelter at the inn. In the interim, very little had changed. The landlady was as stout and brusque as ever, certainly not one they would expect to sit around and talk with the locals. Perhaps if they spoke loudly and dropped tidbits of information, that would be sufficient. By the time dinner hour arrived, they found themselves seated at a table near the window, their clothes relatively dry. Wind-blown rain continued to pelt the leaded glass. Thunder boomed and shook the rafters.

The inn was crowded with those caught unawares by the storm, but the busy activity and many candles and lanterns situated throughout the large dining room gave a festive air to the gathering.

A barmaid approached with twin mugs of porter clutched in her hands.

"Evenin' gents! I daresay you're 'appy to find yourselves indoors this night. Will you take some stew? Boxty made it up fresh yesterday. It'll carry you all the way to Town and it be going fast."

John declined, but Gerhardt requested a large bowl and took both of the beers off her hands.

"Planning on sleeping well tonight?" John asked.

"Like the dead. Or should I say, 'the undead'?" Gerhardt spent the next two minutes draining one of the porters. John gave him a skeptical look.

"I beg you not to drink yourself under the table. Between the two of us, you have me by a whole stone. And I get the feeling no one in this inn is going to be inclined to help me carry you up stairs."

Gerhardt grinned with all his teeth and then returned his attention to the porter.

"Any luck on the code last night, then? You looked frustrated," Gerhardt said.

"No luck and yes, I was frustrated. The clues to the code are there, it's simply a matter of determining what they are. It is the most aggravating thing to feel that one is *almost* upon a discovery, but might as well be a million miles away for the good it does them."

The stew came in an oversize bowl, a giant wooden spoon sunk deep into the thick, brown depths. Gerhardt grinned again.

"Just think, if this is their ordinary ware," Gerhardt said and all but buried his nose in the bowl, "their serving platters must serve a whole regiment."

The smell of it alone was going to make John toss up his accounts. Or at least send him into a round of dry heaving.

"Accept my apologies for refusing to keep you company, but – I assure you – it is in both our interests that I make my way to my bed," John announced. "That 'stew' can't be made with anything resembling beef. I have a nose for these things."

Gerhardt's spoon paused on its way towards his mouth. His eyes dropped to the chunks of meat swimming in the mixture. He shrugged and resumed eating.

"Tell the landlord we want the best. I'm paying," Gerhardt threw over his shoulder as John strode away.

****

John rolled over and resituated his head on his coat. He didn't dare trust the musty, yellowed, cloth-covered mat the landlord had claimed was a pillow. It was bad enough that he had to suffer through the bedbug infested mattress. Why couldn't the stupid creatures tell he had nothing for them? Thunder rolled again, taking on a peculiar rhythm. His sleep be-fogged mind slogged up out of unconsciousness as the pounding continued.

He pulled his head up, confused at the thought that it was coming from his door.

"Gerhardt?" he asked, expecting to hear an answer from the man who slept in the other bed. But there was none. Four porters, two bowls of stew, and one night spent on watch apparently induced a coma in anyone. The pounding continued.

"Coming! Coming. Just a moment, if you please." John stumbled out of the bed. With no dressing gown to relieve his state of partial undress, he wrapped the counterpane around his shoulders in a loose toga that covered most of his bare chest, if not his stocking-less feet.

Squinting as if it would help him navigate his way through the blackness toward the door, he finally found the door, turned the key, and pulled it open.

Miss Isherwood stood in the darkened corridor, a lantern held high in her hand, her hair a sopping wet mess, a pair of men's boots on her feet, and a smile of triumph on her face.

"Miss Isherwood," John began, and then, before he could stop himself, he peered at her more closely. His head snapped up and he focused his eyes on a point above her head. "Beg pardon, I don't mean to, er, stare. But you are wearing a pelisse over your nightgown. This is highly unconventional. If you have any reputation, it's just been thoroughly destroyed. How did you find your way here in this weather?"

"Bother with all that! I figured it out!"

John stared at her. His eyelids were still attempting to remain in their closed, sleeping, position.

"Wake up, Mr. Grissom, do! I had to come tell you. And there's nothing untoward. Your manservant accompanied me."

Her brows bunched together as she had a thought.

"I can't say Moses was enthusiastic about driving me here in the dead of night, especially with the new pony. He was afraid the animal would spook from the thunder, but he handled himself well. The animal that is. And Moses too.

"Anyway, I had hidden the code and notes in my valise before we left your laboratory to introduce Gerhardt to my father – just in case all you gentlemen planned on discussing male interests for several hours. I couldn't sleep tonight so I took it out and started working on it. Here, hold this."

She thrust the lantern at him and rummaged at her feet. John averted his gaze and felt his blood warm. How could she think she could come here, pull up her night gown to her calf to dig around in her father's boots, and he would remain unaffected? He was still a man after all, a creature of flesh, if not of blood.

Eventually she pulled out several sheets of folded paper from the inside of her boot.

"Beg pardon for their sorry state, but I didn't want to risk getting them wet."

"It couldn't wait until tomorrow, Miss Isherwood?"

Miss Isherwood paused in unfolding the papers.

"Well, I suppose it could have. But I couldn't. Come on, then," she said, enjoining him to bring his head closer. "I was thinking about what you were saying about Waite using a decoder device. A book say, or a previous letter. But then I got to thinking, what if the decoder was part of the message." She pointed at the text on the first letter. "Certain of these characters repeat in the same sequence on this page. On this page these characters repeat in a similar repetition. The most common word in the English language is 'the' – if we consider that each page requires its own code, we can see that the letter t, h, and e will each have six different characters, a separate code for each page. Which would explain why there are far too many characters for an alphabet if the characters are taken as a whole."

John took the letter from her and held it up to the light. He should have grabbed his spectacles, but he didn't dare leave the door lest the convention-less Miss Isherwood take into her head to follow him into the room. He held it closer to the lantern, and then held his breath as black lines slowly became visible on the yellowed vellum.

"Are you seeing this?" John asked, holding his breath.

Miss Isherwood stepped up to his shoulder.

"Oh," she breathed.

They both studied it for several seconds more.

"Give me the other one," he said. John held it up to the lantern. Again, thin black lines traced their way under certain sequences of characters.

"Do you have all the letters with you?" he asked.

"No, I left them at the cottage. I only thought to bring these two, so you could compare them."

He handed her the lantern.

"Have Moses take you back to the cottage. I would accompany you myself, but I don't care to risk anyone seeing us together whilst you are in this deplorable state of undress."

"Good grief, Mr. Grissom, you would think I was a woman of loose morals, the way you talk."

"Perhaps not that, but certainly, you have temporarily lost your senses. I shall chalk it up to your enthusiasm. Now, if you please, go. I will work on the letters tomorrow." She turned away from him, her wet braid dripping water down the back of her pelisse. "And tell Moses he can expect an interview with me on the morrow."

She threw him a quelling look over her shoulder. "I suppose to take him to task for bringing me here? I wish you wouldn't."

"I am not in the habit of entertaining unmarried ladies in the dead of night, Miss Isherwood. And you mustn't ever forget what I am, no matter how gentle I may appear. You never know."

She nodded and turned away. John went back into the room, the letters in his hand.

He poked the fire to life and lit a candle. Gerhardt continued to sleep undisturbed, a fact which worried him. Was he so inebriated he was unresponsive? John consoled himself with the thought that perhaps Gerhardt felt such

112

comfort in his presence, his normal heightened awareness was relaxed. After all, the man was only human. John could hardly expect him to be constantly vigilant.

His pocket watch read one in the morning. The hour was late. His eyes fell on the bed. He could use the sleep. The responsible thing to do would be to go back to bed and wake up refreshed, prepared to tackle this new puzzle. But there was no bamming himself, there wasn't a chance he was going back to sleep after Miss Isherwood had brought what was more than likely the key to discovering this whole conundrum.

He pulled out the small table near his bed. It wasn't much as far as work spaces went, but it would have to do.

****

John pinched the corner of his eyebrow to relieve the pain throbbing across his brow and then put his spectacles back on. The lack of sleep was starting to affect him, but with dawn only an hour away and the importance of what he – and Miss Isherwood – had discovered sitting like the world on his shoulders, he knew sleep wasn't in the realm of possibility.

He picked up his watch off the table and checked the time. Six am. Gerhardt could do with a wake-up call. More than eight hours was surely not healthy for a grown man.

"Wake up, Gerhardt." John pulled apart the curtains. It wasn't light enough outside to do much more than tint the room a lighter shade of black, the lit candle notwithstanding. Gerhardt still didn't rouse.

John grabbed the pitcher of water off the table. He stuck his fingers in and flicked water on Gerhardt's face. Gerhardt grumbled and swatted the empty air. He cracked open an eye. His glance fell on the pitcher of water and his eyes flew open. He sat up.

"What are you doing?"

"I did contemplate dumping the pitcher, if you didn't wake up. It's a wonder you've survived this long if you sleep like that."

"Like what?"

"Like the mail coach could have gone through our room at top speed and you wouldn't have noticed."

John held the letters out to him, along with the translations. Gerhardt ceased stretching his limbs and took them.

"What's this?" Gerhardt asked.

"We had a visitor last night. Miss Isherwood discovered that each page has its own code. Hence, I spent the greater part of the morning decoding the letters. Those are the first two, as best as I could make out."

Gerhardt read them silently.

"They are innocuous enough. I take it the underlined words are the actual message?"

John nodded. Gerhardt held the paper closer to the light and began reading the coded message aloud.

"-----th Regiment. At. Dresden – that's the Sixth Coalition – Serum ready by September." Gerhardt looked up at him. "The serum you are working on?"

"I suspect so. He didn't give me a time frame, but if it needs to be ready by September, they will need at least a month to get it to whoever is receiving it on the other side." John shook his head. "Waite told me he could get me a German made microscope lens. I had no idea how."

"And the other one?" Gerhardt asked, reaching for the paper in John's hand.

"Here, I wrote it down on the back. 'Physician Munroe dead. Serum production reassigned. Local militia infiltration complete.' There are several more letters at the cottage."

"Miss Isherwood only brought these two?"

"Yes." John washed his face and combed wet fingers through his unruly hair. It would have to do for a toilette.

114

"And?" Gerhardt wiggled his eyebrows. John stared him down, mustering as much superiority into his arched brow as he could manage.

"And, nothing. I sent her home with a flea in her ear for failing to uphold standards of modesty."

"So you should. Maybe she's taken a liking to you," Gerhardt said. It was a statement but it sounded like a question. John began donning his shirt to cover the confusion he felt at the thought of Miss Isherwood developing warmer feelings for him. For so long he had not allowed himself the pleasure of associating with the softer sex. He couldn't afford to do so now. At least, not socially.

"I remind you she is my assistant, Gerhardt. And I am… diseased." His waistcoat and coat were a sadly crumpled affair, but there was nothing he could do about that.

"I will have to take this to my superiors," Gerhardt announced, waving the letters.

John shook his head and held out his hand.

"I'm afraid I don't know enough about you to trust that you are going to take those to the proper authorities. Give them here. I allowed you a look as a matter of courtesy."

"A pox upon such courtesy." Gerhardt ignored John's hand. "Who do you think the proper authorities are? Who would you take them to?"

"The proper authority is the Crown, of course. Whitehall."

"And how do you plan on managing it? Are you going to waltz into Whitehall, demand an audience with Lord Wellesley, slap the letters on his desk, and denounce Lord Waite as a vampire?"

"Well, no, I-"

"I didn't think so. I assure you, these letters *will* reach Lord Wellesley, current Secretary of the Foreign Office. It is in the best interests of the Crown and England."

"Then you are taking me with you." John was prepared to wrestle the papers from him – and probably fail in the attempt given Gerhardt's size – but he wasn't going to give up the only evidence he had against Waite without a fight.

Gerhardt paused, shrugged, and resumed placing the papers into his satchel. He turned to strap on his belt of vampire hunting paraphernalia that, John had come to believe, he sincerely never went anywhere without.

"Yes. Come with me," Gerhardt said, snugging up the belt and then tying back his hair. "He'll probably require a debriefing from you anyway. Can you decode the remaining papers on the way?"

"Well enough."

John adjusted his spectacles on his nose, and rested against the door. They would have to pick up the papers from the cottage first. And he should probably eat something before his growling stomach pains morphed into something much, much worse. Then it was off on a grand adventure to meet Lord Wellesley.

Although it had required great lengths to subdue his awe at the idea of meeting the head of the Foreign Office, the brother of the famed Arthur Wellesley himself, he was both intimidated and expectant at once. But overriding both emotions was the hope that some sort of action would be taken after the letters were revealed.

Of course, Waite's capture would not be a simple affair. John imagined he would be relegated to the proverbial back room while all of the veteran officers, like Gerhardt, went in with their stakes, and garlic, and silver, and ran the man down in his mansion of horrors and blood slaves. Yes, his adventures were soon to end. Then it would be back to his treatises, and monkeys, and specimen tubes. Would Miss Isherwood care for the drab work once Waite's capture was effected? His spectacles slid down his nose again and he shoved them up with a finger.

116

Gerhardt slid his arms into his skirted, near floor-length, brown leather cape. John decided the cape was a tad dramatic. With one last look at the room, Gerhardt slung the satchel over his shoulder.

"After you, my vision-impaired friend," Gerhardt said.

John walked out the door. If only someone would invent a way to ensure spectacles stayed up. And an easy way to transport tooth powder.

CHAPTER 9

"Please tell me you aren't going to give Moses his walking papers when he only capitulated to my demands after I insisted on his help," Miss Isherwood argued. "He wouldn't have come with me but for the fact that I threatened to go by myself if he didn't provide escort. Yes, it was stupid, I admit. But," she sighed, "like you said, I was carried away with enthusiasm. Surely you can relate. I defy you to tell me you went to sleep after I left last night."

Miss Isherwood glanced up at him. Her eyes were darkened with vehemence. She was in particularly good looks this morning and it was hard to maintain a stern appearance. But he didn't want her to think either a beguiling glance (if that is what she was affecting) or a brow beating would force him to roll over so easily, as if he had no backbone. If he let her think it was so easy to talk him out of things, she might do something as foolish again. He deepened his unyielding countenance, aided by his spectacles which, as usual, were beginning to descend down his nose.

"Oh, no. You are going to do it, aren't you," she said. "If you release him from your employ, I am hiring him at my father's Town house. It's been too long since we've had a servant there."

John ducked under a tree branch that had grown across the path. Now that her father was living here – and he didn't know for how long – Moses would need to tend the grounds more than he was accustomed to. The small kitchen garden was a raucous wilderness of herbs and shrubbery. Thyme and rosemary spilled over onto the stone pathway. Hedge rows of marjoram and overgrown sage had burst their once manicured squares and ovals to bunch up in some places and gape in others. He knew the old surgeon preferred the

118

outdoors. This place could be quite welcoming were Moses to put some time and effort into it.

"Mr. Grissom?"

"Beg pardon. You have caught me wool gathering. How will you pay him?" John asked. "You are barely making enough to keep yourself out of the weeds."

"I am sure he will be happy just to have a roof over his head. We will figure out a payment fee later. Or I will help him find a better position as soon as I am able."

John couldn't help but admire her determination. She couldn't know he had already spoken with Moses and that the man was definitely staying on. But it touched him to realize her sense of honor was keen enough to demand that he place the blame on her, rather than Moses. Nevertheless, it was time to put her out of her misery.

"No. I am not going to send him packing. He has been a most reliable steward of this property for the past five years. I won't throw that away on one faulty decision."

"Pfft. What could the man have done?"

"To someone who suggests riding out in a storm, in the dead of night, with no moon? Lock you in your room? Hide the saddles? Lock the barn? Tie you to a chair? Is there anything that would have been so awful for which your father and I would not have been in his debt? You do realize that had the storm washed out the bridge, we could have lost you both? I can't imagine your father took the news of your midnight escapade with any more equanimity than I did."

Miss Isherwood ducked her head down, her cheeks rosy with remorse.

"He was not happy. And he was questioning the prudence of allowing me to continue working with you. Until I talked him out of it." She looked up at him and pursed her lips. "I am embarrassed to think your concern is due to my childish indiscretion."

119

"Yes. Well." John cleared his throat. This cravat was going to strangle him. "I wonder myself whether we should rethink this arrangement. Should I have to worry that you will make such an unthinking decision in the future?"

"No, of course not." Her voice began to take on an edge. "But I've said I am sorry backward and forward. I know it was rash. What more can I do to convince you that it won't happen again? I know it seems like I have less care for my reputation than I do – and to be honest, perhaps I have become less sensitive to censure because of my having to be as independent as I have been – but I do care about it.

"I haven't had the luxury of being taken about in society or protected from the rougher elements, though my father did what he could. In all sincerity, I don't know if I would want to be protected in that manner. So maybe that contributes as well, I don't know." She shrugged her shoulders and shook her head. "I only know working with you has been invigorating. Well, except for cleaning up after the monkeys and rats. I really feel like I am doing something for mankind, for the future. For my father. Please don't give up on me. And do consider, the storm was mostly gone."

"It was raining."

"It was sprinkling."

"You looked like a drowned rat." John stopped and ground his teeth together. He had gone too far. "I beg your pardon, Miss Isherwood. That was unmannerly of me."

Miss Isherwood took a deep breath and let it out slowly. "Apology accepted."

John began walking again, the young woman whose hand nestled in the crook of his elbow taking up his thoughts. There were things about Miss Isherwood that spoke to him in ways he couldn't contemplate too deeply. That scared him. But she was a wonderful assistant. She had taken two hours each day to work through his treatises, cataloguing them according to subject, and then alphabetizing them. His scrawling hand hadn't prevented her from taking on the task of copying his journal entries into a legible hand. She had come to him with several related entries she thought bore further inspection, and recommended that others be compiled into a paper and presented to the Medico society. Altogether, she had more than proven her usefulness. Of course he would keep her on.

"I won't give up on you," John said. "For a variety of reasons. To give credit where it is due, I have been impressed with your work. I perhaps do not say it often enough. And there is your situation to consider as well. Regardless of your sex, I am not inclined to remove the income from a person who is the sole support of their parent."

Her eyes started to gleam with unshed tears. John silently offered her his handkerchief.

"You've done so much already," she said. "Thank you."

"That's quite enough of that crying on my shoulder. Your father is likely looking down at us from the window. He'll wonder what's made you a watering pot. Stop it now, or you'll ruin my glossy Hessians with that flood."

She threw the handkerchief at him.

"You are ridiculous. I wasn't even crying." She moved away toward the house. "And your Hessians, if they are that, lost their gloss long before I watered up."

Part of the garden had been wrecked in the storm. The walk, littered with branches and leaves, had petals from the summer roses blown about so that a thin carpet of pink spotted the stones.

"As soon as I get the letters from you, Miss Isherwood, I'll be going. You may stay with your father until it is safe to remove him back to Town."

"I beg pardon?" she asked, stopping abruptly. "Why am I not returning to Town? I can hardly fulfill the role of assistant if I am here."

He offered her his arm and they continued at a slow walk toward the house.

"True, but another day won't hurt anything. I am accompanying Gerhardt to meet with his employer to show him the letters and – "

"I am holding them hostage."

John sighed.

"You are not holding them hostage. I am taking the letters. You are staying here. I don't want to have to worry about you."

"What is it you think I am going to do? You may drop me off at the laboratory. Did you even consider who would take care of your poor animals? They haven't eaten since yesterday morning the poor things. Just think, Monkey #57, or whatever his number is, has probably already flung his dung all over the other creatures."

John drew up short, aghast at the realization that she was right. How could he have been so thoughtless? It was one thing to use them for testing purposes – that was to the benefit of humanity. It was another to let them suffer needlessly.

"He does get dreadfully bad tempered if he's hungry, doesn't he?" John admitted.

"Speaking of which, are you sure you didn't accidentally jab him with a needle filled with your blood. That might explain his foul temper when he hasn't eaten." Miss Isherwood buttoned up her lip.

"Quite the quiz this morning, aren't we, Miss Isherwood." And then, because he couldn't hold it in, he laughed.

They entered the house with smiles on their faces, but it was a somber pair they found in the study, pouring over the remaining letters.

"Did you get those out of my room?" Miss Isherwood cried.

"I took the liberty of searching them out, yes," Gerhardt said. "Only after I asked your father for permission to find them."

Mr. Isherwood cringed. "I didn't realize you would even consider invading my daughter's privacy, Mr. Van Helsing. Apologies, Henrietta."

"There goes your bargaining chip," John said in an aside to her.

"Monkeys!" she whispered back.

"Now," John clapped his hands and looked over Mr. Isherwood's shoulder. "What has the two of you looking so grim on this bright June day?"

They both turned to look at him, puzzlement on their faces. He supposed that he *had* done it a bit too brown. They turned back to the decoded letters. Gerhardt picked up a sheet of the translations and handed it to him.

"Read for yourself."

John pushed his spectacles up again.

"*Army. –th Regiment inoculation set for May 12. Brighton.* 'May 12.' That's in two days!"

"So it is."

"Whatever the inoculation is for, it can't be good. Can it be?" Miss Isherwood asked.

Gerhardt shook his head.

"If this were legitimate troop business, our resident bacteriologist here wouldn't have overheard Waite discussing them replacing the inoculation batch. Nor would Waite be sending word of it across the sea through secret channels."

"It isn't possible that whoever he answers to is on the Continent?"

"Perhaps. There is this one as well," Gerhardt said, handing him another sheet.

"*Will oversee personally. London regiment failed. Will schedule for new inoculation to take place in two weeks.* 'Will oversee personally,'" John repeated. "The Brighton inoculations. He'll be there, then?"

"From what I gather," Gerhardt said.

"Then we can stop him."

"Won't it look suspicious? Their dispensing inoculations at night, I mean?" Miss Isherwood asked.

"No, anything that comes down the official channels, especially *this* official channel, may be met with disgruntlement, but it won't be questioned," Gerhardt said.

"Anything else?" John asked, dreading the answer. He couldn't conceive of how much worse things could get.

"That's as much as we've been able to translate so far," Mr. Isherwood said. "But Mr. Van Helsing tells me you will be translating on the way there. You must take my portable writing desk," he continued, on seeing John's nod.

"We won't have time to discuss the letters with Lord Wellesley as planned. Not until after Brighton is dealt with, assuming we can address it."

"Can you hire Bow St. Runners at least, to aid you?" Miss Isherwood asked. She was looking increasingly nervous.

"I'm afraid not. We will have to leave immediately if we want to make Brighton by noon the day of."

"The stable near my quarters has reliable hacks for hire," John offered.

"No. I've a mind to acquire us faster steeds," Gerhardt grinned, which made John wonder what exactly he was planning.

"Your daughter volunteered to go with us, at least as far as the laboratory," John turned to the older vampire. "I have testing animals that require feeding and care."

"Good heavens! Wild animals! None of them are diseased, are they?" Mr. Isherwood exclaimed.

124

"No, not yet. But when I am experimenting on them, I assure you we take the greatest precautions."

"Indeed, Papa," Miss Isherwood said, waving her fingers at him. "My hands will be quite ruined before long for all the scrubbing and dipping in and out of alcohol solutions I have to do to please him."

"Who cares about hands? I'd much rather have you alive, Henrietta," her father said.

"You will be well without me, won't you, father?" Miss Isherwood asked, taking both of her father's hands. "No more episodes? You have Betsy, so if you start feeling the slightest bit peckish, just do like John showed you and take some of her blood. She has plenty of water and food, so I can't imagine that you could take more than she could give."

"Impossible," John reassured.

Mr. Isherwood kissed his daughter on the cheek and then stepped back.

"Off with you now. And no more stunts like the one you pulled last night. You're far too old for me to be worrying about in that fashion."

John shook Mr. Isherwood's hand and thanked him for his well wishes before following Miss Isherwood's slim, navy draped form out the door to the waiting carriage. If everything went according to plan, Gerhardt and he would have a grueling ride ahead of them. They would reach Brighton a mere half-day before the inoculations were set to take place. That would leave them, at best six to eight hours to find their quarry and stop the switch. He longed to take advantage of the twenty minutes on the way into Town to sleep, but with the translations waiting for him to complete, he knew that would be impossible.

The writing desk was brought out to them and then they were off. Miss Isherwood sat next to him on the bench seat while opposite, Gerhardt tipped his hat forward and made himself as comfortable as he could get given the limited space and his belt-ful of equipment.

John and Miss Isherwood worked on the remaining translations together. With only minutes remaining before the carriage pulled onto Griffin St. and no fire to warm the vellum and show even a single message, they were at a disappointing loss.

John rubbed his fingers through his hair, frustration gripping him. They were so close! Suddenly, he realized he knew a way to get heat onto the vellum. He turned the vellum character side down on the closed writing desk.

"Start rubbing, Miss Isherwood. You there, Gerhardt!" John slapped his knee. "Help us. Rub until your fingers start burning. All over. Pick small spots."

They all began rubbing the paper, their fingers rapidly moving back and forth.

"Why are we doing this?" Gerhardt asked.

"So we can see the message."

"That's idiotic. Why didn't you ask if I had a match?" Gerhardt asked and then dug into his pocket. "As it happens, I have several."

John rolled his eyes and took the matches from him. The match flared to life. He carefully held it to the underside of the paper and watched as the once invisible lines darkened across the page. The match began to warm his fingertips and he dropped it the floor. Gerhardt was already lighting another when the first few drips of blood began hitting the parchment.

"Stop. We have it," John said, throwing back his head and grabbing for his handkerchief. "Miss Isherwood, if you would be so kind as to crack the carriage window, I would be much obliged."

"Are you dying?" Gerhardt asked, bafflement evident in his voice.

"No," John said around the handkerchief. "I'm afraid the closed confines have exacerbated the sulphuric effects of the matches, which in turn induced a nose bleed."

"In that case," Gerhardt slid the parchment off his lap and proceeded to work through the message. "'New physician working on serum. John Grissom. V. Hired assistant Henrietta Isherwood. H. will remove when appropriate.'"

Silence filled the carriage, but for the sounds coming in through the windows. The sunlight, so cheery and warm before, now seemed harsh and cold. Miss Isherwood swallowed and ducked her head.

"What do you suppose the 'H' means?" An odd tremble took her voice as the question left her lips.

"Human," Gerhardt replied.

CHAPTER 10

"These are prime bloods!" John said. His mouth dropped open in awe at the creatures dancing before him on the pea gravel. Gerhardt held them with ease.

"Indeed. Racing horses, actually." Gerhardt waved away the hackney driver who, after the generous payment Gerhardt had provided, had been happy to stand and wait for thirty minutes to make sure Gerhardt's attempt to procure mounts for them proved successful. When they had first arrived at the house, John was duly impressed by the connections Gerhardt cultivated. To call it a house was, in fact, an understatement of the residence. With two wings that flanked a central trunk, a Georgian façade interrupted with rows of glass windows through which he could see portrait galleries, and more chimneys dotting its roof than the entire row of town houses on --------- street in Mayfair, it was an estate home of the first stare.

John gave him a questioning look, speechless in response to Gerhardt's race horse assertion.

"The owner owed me a favor."

"Does he know we'll almost be killing his steeds in taking them to Brighton?"

"We won't be pressing them that hard. I think you underestimate the difference in speed between a hired hack and one of these beauties." Gerhardt stroked the nose of the nearer stallion.

"So, in other words, no. He doesn't know." John acquainted himself with his own mount and then swung himself up into the saddle. "The local constable will likely think we've stolen them. Look at us."

Gerhardt favored him with a wolfish grin.

"Not me, they won't. I have papers. I don't know what you're going to do." He sprang his horse.

"Wait. What's that you say?" John asked, following on his own a second later. The rushing of the wind over the pounding of hooves drowned out any answer.

****

Brighton's Crescent was busy with activity, but John was almost falling out of the saddle with fatigue. He was pleased to see Gerhardt wasn't faring much better.

John had fed the night before, knowing that once they were in Brighton he wouldn't have access to fresh blood. Hunting for live animals without normal vampire skills made it much more difficult, but with time he had improved his abilities. Catching the deer last night had involved a technique of flushing and shooting – a dangerous enterprise in the dead of night – but it had proved successful. The animal had sated him, and then, when he had had his fill, he passed the deer off to Gerhardt who broke down a haunch and roasted it, and then fired the remainder. Wasting the meat was not ideal, but at least they had made some use of it.

The sun was high in the sky when they entered the sea-side town. His watch read shortly before noon. Both of them were covered in dirt from their travels and longed for a hot bath and sleep, but it was not to be had. Somewhere in Brighton, Waite and his men were preparing to switch out the batch of vaccines for something that could prove lethal – or worse. Unless it was already done.

"We need to find the barracks," John said.

"Church Street."

John looked over at him. "Is there anything you don't know?"

"In my experience, knowledge of places is pivotal.... And I may have been in a position of needing to know this information before."

John snorted. They found Church St. and followed it to the barracks. The massive buildings took up long stretches of land and red-coated army regulars roved to and fro, horses standing in front of the Georgian fronted barracks, pawing the dust. In a field next to the street, foot soldiers conducted reviews, their lieutenants barking out the commands.

"How are we going to find out where they are keeping their inoculations?" John asked.

"The quartermaster should have them. Or the Surgeon's Office."

"We can't just ask."

"No, but I wanted to ride through and see if there was any unusual activity. I should also speak with the barrack's commander."

"About what?"

"I want papers from him showing that he is aware we are on the property on the Crown's business."

John smiled.

"Does that make me an officer of the Crown?" he asked.

A beat passed before Gerhardt answered, trying to bite back a grin.

"If you like," Gerhardt said. "I never thought to see the day when my lord Wellesley could find himself in the position of paying a vampire for services rendered."

A dragoon on horseback rode within hailing distance of them.

"Beg pardon, sergeant," Gerhardt called out. "Would you kindly give us the direction to your commander's office?"

Moments later they were alighting from their mounts. John felt like his legs would buckle. The feeling in them began to return after several steps, but the ache remained.

"I am going to need an extremely hot soak in a tub after this is over," he said.

"Maybe we could avail ourselves of a groom and get rubbed down."

John frowned and looked over at Gerhardt.

"Do they do that sort of thing?"

"No. I imagine that's more the responsibility of a valet. But I figure it's worth a try."

They came to a stop outside the door of the barrack commander's office. Gerhardt smoothed back long hair that had done its best to escape its queue, but attempting to make themselves appear presentable was impossible. The door was opened by an adjutant who took a glance at travel stained clothes and proceeded to ignore the formalities.

"Do you have an appointment?"

"Good afternoon, Captain. You may give your commander this," Gerhardt said, handing him a narrow, leather-bound portfolio. "We'll wait."

The captain took it from Gerhardt.

"No guarantees that he'll see you. He's very busy."

"He'll see me."

The adjutant shrugged and opened the door to allow them into an ante-room. A desk stood in one corner, files and documents stacked in sharp rows.

"Have a seat, sirs."

The adjutant opened another door and closed it behind him. John tried not to listen to the muted voices, but his acute hearing couldn't prevent his hearing the commander's outrage that some commoner would demand an audience. The captain's defense was followed by silence, rustling, and then the commander demanding that they be shown in immediately.

The captain came out the door, a deferential look on his face. John filed after Gerhardt into the room.

"You may leave us, Holman," the commander said, coming forward to meet them. He brushed self-consciously at his uniform as if he was expecting an inspection. They waited for the door to shut behind the aide. John took that moment to look about himself.

The room was comfortably established as a study, with bookshelves holding treatises on military history and strategy taking up one wall, and a bust of King George III holding court over Dresden miniatures of soldiers and cavalry standing above the empty hearth. The commander's massive desk was evenly balanced against the space in the room, there being a whole fifteen feet to cross before one could seat himself in the twin chairs sitting in front of the desk.

"Colonel. Gerhardt Van Helsing, and my... associate, Mr. John Grissom, Surgeon, at your service," Gerhardt introduced himself with a short, very Prussian, bow from the waist and a crisp, heel click. The colonel held out a hand. He was a man of medium height, once athletic, but now running to fat. His features were marked by folds, as much from poor living and age as from what John theorized was a disposition given to anger.

"Colonel Hugh Duncan. What brings you to Brighton, Mr. Van Helsing?" Duncan asked as they shook hands. "Please, sit."

He led the way toward his desk and rubbed his hands together as if nervous. Although Duncan took up a position behind his desk, none of them sat.

"It is unusual for us receive a visit from the Foreign Office," the colonel said.

Gerhardt took the satchel off his shoulder and produced the packet of translated letters. John had managed to finish their translations while en route, taking advantage of every rest they took to spread them out on any available surface. The last two translations were not neat renditions, but they would suffice. Gerhardt thumped the letters down on the desk in front of Duncan.

John leaned over to the vampire hunter as the colonel began reading the papers.

"I thought you said we weren't going to do this…?"

"Do what?"

"I believe the exact words were, 'waltz in, demand an audience with whoever is in charge, slap the letters on his desk and denounce Lord Waite.'"

"I never said *I* wasn't going to do it. I just asked if that was what you were going to do."

John narrowed his eyes. Gerhardt stared back at him innocently before facing the colonel whose attention remain fixed on the papers. Gerhardt continued, sotto voce, "I suppose I did fail to mention I have a special pass that gives me entrance near anywhere in government."

"You aren't even British."

"No need to look so horrified, John. England's allied with Prussia. And our soldiering is superior."

John set up a round of coughing to cover Gerhardt's blunder. One would think a man of his abilities had more discretion. But Colonel Duncan, who now lifted his eyes from the papers, was thankfully preoccupied with more weighty matters.

"This is tonight!"

"Yes," Gerhardt said.

Duncan dropped the letters on the desk.

"Where did these come from? Where were they going?"

"No need to know," Gerhardt said. "The only part you do need to know concerns whichever of your regiments are receiving those inoculations."

"It mentions you by name, Mr. Grissom. I suppose it would be futile to ask how you are mixed up in this."

John gave a succinct nod.

"We must alert the Surgeon, the Quartermaster," Duncan said.

"No, I don't want to sound a general alarm," Gerhardt said. "That will be sure to let them know the game is afoot.

I just need the paperwork sent round to ensure Mr. Grissom and I may work unencumbered by legalities."

The colonel nodded. "Of course, of course. Whatever you require. Are you sure you don't require militia support?" Duncan looked John over doubtfully.

"Impossible," Gerhardt affirmed. Unless they were armed with wooden stakes or silver bullets, John thought to himself.

"When were the vaccines supposed to arrive?" John asked.

"You'll have to ask the quartermaster. My adjutant can provide you with directions, but —" The colonel glanced over at the ormolu clock sitting on the mantel. "I hardly think you'll be able to prevent the switch if they have already arrived. "

Gerhardt headed for the door.

"The inoculations aren't for any of the regiments here, anyhow," Duncan called after him. Gerhardt paused and turned back. "They are for the 10th Hussars."

"The King's Own. Where are they?"

"Preston Barracks. We thought it was odd that the orders scheduled the inoculations for so late in the evening."

"There are reasons for it." Gerhardt turned back for the door. "Come, Grissom. And Colonel, if you would send the paperwork around immediately, I would be most appreciative."

John gave a clipped bow and hurried after Gerhardt.

"That was rather high-handed of you," John muttered while they waited for the adjutant to return with the paperwork and instructions from Duncan.

"I will always take every opportunity to put a blustering officer in his place. Too many of them are bloated with self-importance."

"Here comes the captain," John smiled at the adjutant stepping through the door, "don't hold back now."

"Here are the papers you requested, and if you will follow me, I'll take you down to the quartermaster's office. I understand you are looking for a shipment of vaccines?"

An unsettling silence followed the question. Who else would the colonel tell of the specifics of their mission?

"We are here on the Crown's business, Captain Holman. May we depend on your discretion? Quite possibly the fate of the nation hangs upon it," John said.

The adjutant's face reddened. His back straightened defensively.

"Of course," he said. "Please follow me."

They followed the adjutant down a series of corridors, crossed through a courtyard and entered another building. A red-coated regular on watch snapped a salute at the door holding a plaque that read, "Quartermaster."

The adjutant entered without knocking. An anteroom holding high tables for sorting equipment opened onto a larger room through a window cutout in the wall. An ironbound door was off to one side of the window. Through the grilled cutout, John could see rows and rows of shelving holding blankets, boxes, crates, and stacks of red coats. Behind the desk on the other side of the window a red-coated officer sat making notations into a series of log books.

"Yes?" The officer didn't bother glancing up from his books.

"Ho, Hezwit. Is Walker in?"

Hezwit, a sharp featured young man, sighed heavily and looked up at Holman. He pointed with his pen. "In the back office. Do you require him?"

"No, we will deal with him personally. We need access to the supply room. Colonel's orders."

"I'll need to see them."

Gerhardt slid the papers through the bars. Seconds later, Hezwit handed them back and rose to lift the wooden arm from across the door.

135

"Come on, then. You know how he feels about anyone interfering with his beloved warehouse."

"Oh, he won't like it," Holman said with a wink. "We'll be sure to do it proper."

Holman led them through the maze of shelves to an open door. Inside, a man studied what appeared to be an architectural map, laid out on a table. Pencil markings, smudges, and the scars of removed writing scraped from the vellum covered the whole. John looked at it more closely and realized it was a systematic layout charting the shelves in the warehouse. Holman stopped before the desk and saluted

"Good afternoon, sir. Colonel's orders, sir." Holman handed over a sheet of paper. John assumed it demanded the officer aid Gerhardt and himself in whatever capacity they deemed necessary. The quarter master read the papers, a sour look crossing his mouth. He returned Holman's salute.

"Dismissed, Captain."

"Gentlemen," Holman said, and gave a bow in farewell.

"What do you need?" the quartermaster asked curtly.

"Lieutenant... Walker, is it?" Gerhardt asked. Lieutenant Walker stiffened. Even his gold fringe seemed to stand on end. Over the period of a few moments, his face suffused with red to the very roots of his carefully queued hair.

"Since when does the Crown employ foreigners in its business?" the lieutenant bit out.

"Ah, I see my accent gives me away." Gerhardt shrugged carelessly. John, on the other hand, thought his head might explode.

"I hardly think that is your affair, Lieutenant," John said, taking a step forward. How could anyone have the audacity to question orders from his commander, based off a man's accent alone? Gerhardt waved a calming hand at him.

"The good major's reticence is understandable, Grissom. One can never be too careful. Lieutenant Walker, you'll notice that the orders you received are from Colonel Duncan. If you find these are not compelling enough to open your warehouse to our perusal, perhaps orders from the Foreign Office would be sufficient? Of course, given the nature of our business, it is quite possible you will put an entire regiment of men at risk should we have to wait. And that couldn't possibly please your commanding officer."

John turned to Gerhardt, speechless. Where was this largesse when they were in the colonel's office?

Moments passed before Walker seemed to arrive at a decision.

"No," Walker slapped the orders down. "Never let it be said that I didn't do my duty by King and Country. What do you need?"

"A shipment of vaccines was scheduled to arrive today. Have they?"

Walker wiped a hand over his mouth in thought.

"Yes. About an hour ago. Why?"

"We'll need to see them. We believe someone may have tampered with or will tamper with them," John said.

"If they are safe, we will need to set a guard detail of at least six on them," Gerhardt added.

"Six?! They are armed with muskets," Walker objected. "I hardly think anyone would be fool enough to storm the barracks and steal a crate of medicines."

Gerhardt raised his eyebrows.

"Not steal them, Lieutenant, replace them."

"Oh. I see."

"Oh, indeed. Now, your colonel tells me the vaccines are for the 10th Hussars at the Preston Barracks. Have they already been sent to the barrack surgeon in Preston?"

"Yes. If we can, we disperse items immediately if they are needed locally. I don't care to waste the space in my warehouse."

"Naturally." Gerhardt turned to John. "Shall we? Lewes Street awaits."

John followed Gerhardt out the door, but then paused and stuck his head back in the room.

"Discretion is the better part of valor."

Walker frowned at him in puzzlement. John shook his head and rolled his eyes.

"Keep what you know to yourself. We don't want to tip our hand. If our quarry escapes, I should hate to discover that the reason why could be traced back to you, Lieutenant."

Without waiting for Walker's agreement, John ran after Gerhardt.

"What's on Lewes Street?" John asked as he came abreast of him.

Gerhardt looked over at him.

"Why, Preston Barracks, of course."

John shrugged.

"Of course," he said.

CHAPTER 11

"It's said Preston Barracks can stable over 1,000 horses."

"That is a prodigious amount of cavalry," John said.

Gerhardt nodded and nudged his stallion forward among the supply wagons, carts, and off-duty dragoons who were using the main thoroughfare of Preston Village. With their dirt still on them, groaning as they stepped up into their saddles, John had had to call upon his reserves to make it the short ride to Preston without tumbling to the ground.

He was definitely not up for searching all over the barracks for this surgeon. Late afternoon had started to draw out the supper crowd and red-breasted soldiers strolled the length and breadth of the street, giggling yeoman's daughters dressed in their evening finest on their arms.

"You'd think it was Vauxhall with all the activity here this evening," John murmured. His eyes caught and held on a sign attached to a large, three story, Tudor-styled house.

John pulled on the reins of his mare.

"Gerhardt," he called, pointing. The black painted sign was inscribed with gold lettering: "Maj. Harrison, Royal Army Surgeon's Office." A red door was offset by the cheery glow of light streaming through wide windows. Twilight was coming on fast as the sun began to sink toward the horizon. It made John tired just to look at the place.

Gerhardt clicked his tongue at the stallion and joined John at the gate to the short yard which fronted the building. A glance around them revealed nothing untoward, so they dismounted and went up the walk. Muted sounds of revelry made their way through the door.

"Party," Gerhardt said, and pounded on the door. "Nothing like a drunken surgeon to save your life."

John shrugged. "Surgeons need to recreate too."

The door creaked open. A solemn-faced manservant stood within. Behind him in a large hall-like room, dancers wove in and out in unceasing streams. Shouts of laughter and the lilting strains of fiddle and pipe accompanied them.

"We are here to see Major Harrison. On the King's business," Gerhardt announced.

The servant held the door open for them to enter and gestured to a long, padded bench just inside the door and then left them.

"I can't sit down," John said. "If I do, I won't get back up."

Gerhardt sat down. His toe started tapping to the music. A graying, trimly built officer moved toward them, his dress uniform an eye-catching contrast to the dimly lit confines of the room. He carried the last vestiges of a good time in the smile on his face, but it faded as he approached.

"I'm Major Harrison," he said.

Gerhardt made the introductions again, they shook hands, and then the major led them into an adjoining room lined with books. Despite himself, John's eyes rested on their titles until Gerhardt elbowed him in the ribs.

"Rather than explain why we are here, it'll be easier if you read these." Van Helsing laid his orders and the letters on the table.

They waited silently while the doctor read them, his countenance aghast as he approached the end.

"I'm a surgeon myself, so I know these moments of diversion are rare," John said. "I'm afraid we will be ruining your evening, but it can't be helped."

The major laid the papers on the desk, adjusting them as he thought, until their corners lined up exactly.

"We have the vaccines," the surgeon frowned. "They are scheduled to be given tonight at eleven pm. The orders I received were quite specific on that point."

"May we see a copy of the orders?"

The Major rifled through a desk drawer and then handed over a piece of paper.

"If the writer of these letters is here tonight," Harrison resumed. "I assume we intend on taking him into custody. The question remains, do we wait for the replacement to be made and catch him in the act, or do we put a guard detail on the vaccines and hope we can apprehend him en route?"

"The more sure way to apprehend him – or them, more likely – is to lie in wait," Gerhardt said.

"Why don't we do both?" John asked. "Take the vaccines out of their crates, hide them in different crates elsewhere, and put a guard detail on them. Since I am a surgeon, you may dispense with whatever attendants you were going to use if it comes down to the hour and no one has attempted to replace them. Not that I don't trust your men, but it's possible he's paid off some of them to look the other way."

The major pinched his lips and nodded.

"I suppose I should get rid of my guests."

"Actually, no, not yet. Anything out of the ordinary would be suspicious. You might not enjoy yourself for the rest of the evening, but we'll need you to pretend like you do," Gerhardt said.

"I would be more comfortable if Van Helsing and I removed the vaccines on our own. The less people who know about what is taking place, the better," John said.

"If that is what you wish to do, I suppose I cannot stop you."

"Where are they?"

"Medical Supply, at the other end of the house," the major said and then led the way out of the room.

"You keep them here?" John asked in surprise.

"All the supplies for the barracks. The last thing I need is some fool guard selling laudanum on the sly."

They skirted the main room and went up a short flight of stairs to a high-ceilinged gallery. Curtain covered windows lined its length, but through some that were partially open, John could see that twilight was upon them. Beds empty of all but one or two patients lay on either side beneath oil paintings of austere faced men and women.

"You don't have a separate army hospital then?" John asked.

The major led the way through the beds to a door at the end.

"No, there hasn't been any need for one." He took a small ring of keys off his hip and unlocked the door. It revealed a small room crowded with tables, tubs, and various other equipment, but no crates. He picked up a branch of candles near the door and lit them. The gloom in the gallery was sure to give way to blackness in the confines of a storage room. A door inset in one wall read 'Medical Supply.' He unlocked this as well and led them inside.

John started. A corpse lay on a table in the front of the room. John grabbed Gerhardt's arm to stop him.

"Major?" Gerhardt asked with a tense nod toward the body.

"Oh, him. He must have died recently. Our undertaker refuses to take bodies after four in the afternoon."

"And you are sure he is dead?" Gerhardt asked.

"Of course. Look at him." All of them studied the man's pale features and the arms crossed across his chest. John listened intently but detected no heartbeat.

"Was he a patient?" John asked.

"I assume so. He's wearing the night shirt we provide our patients with. I'm not in the habit of caring for patients who are not in immediate need of my services."

John looked at the corpse and then back at the surgeon.

"It looks like he might have been in need of your services. Just hazarding a thought."

The major shrugged.

"Perhaps he died unexpectedly so they didn't feel the need to call me. I suppose I should confirm that he actually is dead. My nurse is normally trustworthy, but the fact that I didn't know about him is odd. "

He set the candelabra down, pushed aside the opening to the white night shirt and laid his ear on the man's chest. Gerhardt glanced over at John and discretely undid the buttons on his coat. He gave John a questioning look. But John shrugged.

There was no way of knowing whether the man was a vampire. Their heartbeats were so infrequent and low there was no guarantee John would hear it. Exposing the body to garlic or some other allergen was the only sure way to discover whether it was a vampire.

Which is exactly what Gerhardt was going to do, John realized, as he watched Gerhardt pull out the stopper on a refreshed vial of garlic water. John sneezed loudly. The major turned to them and opened his mouth to speak. Behind him, the corpse's eyes flew open.

"Major," Gerhardt bit out. "Move. Now."

But rather than moving, the Major Harrison turned to look over his shoulder. He started in fright as the vampire's fingers clutched him around the neck, his fangs fully extended. The Major was paralyzed in the vampire's grip. Gerhardt ran forward and dumped what he could of the vial onto the vampire's head. The drops sizzled on the pale skin. The vampire howled and Gerhardt used his moment of distraction to rip the major out of his grasp.

The vampire jumped to the floor, landing in a crouch.

"John! The candles!" Gerhardt shouted. From his belt, Gerhardt pulled out a slim five inch silver stake – John saw that he had a whole row of them strapped diagonally across his front - and a mallet. John grabbed the candelabra, wishing that it were a torch instead. What were the odds of them being able to start an unrestrained vampire on fire with some puny candles?

The vampire hissed at them, his red eyes coming to a stop on John.

"Traitor!"

Almost faster than the eye could see, the vampire launched himself at John. John waved the flaming candles before him, slowing the vampire down. The vampire looked every bit the part of a Bedlam escapee with the nightgown swaying about his knees.

Gerhardt leapt forward with his stake and mallet. The vampire turned and backhanded him out of the air, crushing him to the floor. Harrison backed up against shelving lining the wall, his face drained of blood. The vampire turned back to John.

He stalked him, remaining out of reach of the fire. Gerhardt began to revive from his position on the floor. The vampire smiled at John. He reached down and dragged Gerhardt up from the floor with one hand around his neck. While Gerhardt was taller, he was no match for the vampire's strength. He slammed a fist into the vampire's cheek, but it made no more of an impression than to nudge the vampire's head to one side.

John ran up and set as many flaming candle tips onto back of the vampire's night shirt as possible. The vampire dropped Gerhardt and slapped at the flames, but the damage was done. The shirt went from smoking to engulfing the vampire in flames in all of a minute. The horrible screams and howls turned into groans and moans as the fire burned, until, as if the undead corpse was at last giving way to its deficiencies, it began crumbling to dust from the outside in.

The flames died leaving them in near pitch black darkness. A match struck, and the Major, with shaking hands, lit the candelabra again. Gerhardt sat on the floor hacking and drawing in deep breaths. John opened the door to air the room, wondering what the few patients in the gallery must be thinking of what they had heard.

Major Harrison approached the spot where the vampire had burnt up. A body-shaped pile of coal colored dust was all that remained.

144

"I don't even know... what to... how did you...?" the major asked, raising his eyes from the floor.

"Need... to know," Gerhardt gasped.

"We can tell you he was part of the conspiracy," John said.

The major rubbed his bruised neck and nodded.

"Yes, I gathered that."

****

The last of the crates had been emptied. Field size bottles of alcohol had been put in their place and re-covered with straw packing before the lids were hammered back into place. John slumped over onto a crate of vaccines. He was so tired. He took off his spectacles and rubbed his eyes. They stung from lack of sleep.

They had only a few more hours, if that, before the scheduled hour came. Was it too much to hope that they had overcome the culprit? Granted, Waite had declared in the letter that he would see to it personally, but did that mean he actually would? Or was he yet lurking in the town, waiting for them to leave the house, move toward the inoculation area, and then perform a switch en route?

The King's Own were to be gathered together on the parade grounds next to the barracks. The move thus required a horse and wagon, along with the injection paraphernalia. As per his protocol safety codes, John had demanded a bucket of high proof alcohol be ready at the site. He didn't want to run the risk of sharing diseases between the cavalrymen any more than was already going to happen.

The major had returned to his residence, shaken from the ordeal. Gerhardt had accompanied him, John assumed to provide an explanation for what he had witnessed – though what plausible, reasonable, explanation Gerhardt would offer he had no clue.

145

Footsteps sounded in the gallery without. John picked up his head, waiting. His shoulders sagged in relief as he glimpsed Gerhardt's rugged form striding toward him between the beds. By the time Gerhardt was in the small staging room, John was recovered.

"No visitors?"

"Other than the ones already here?" John asked, referencing several patients who lay half-traumatized with fright in the gallery. "We really should have insisted they be moved given the danger of this operation."

Gerhardt nodded and then hefted a non-vaccine crate over one shoulder, its wood sides labeled with red stamped letters: INOCULATIONS.

"Too late. The cart is here and we're moving these out now."

"What about these?" John asked, patting the real vaccines.

"We're taking all of them in two different carts. The cart with these," Gerhardt patted the red-labeled box on his shoulder, "will take the expected route. Those will take a longer route to the staging area."

"If he recognizes us, will he suspect a switch?" John asked, taking up a crate himself.

"Perhaps. Perhaps he'll think we are just guarding them."

Gerhardt carried his crate down the gallery to meet the guards who would accompany them. John gagged as a blanket fog of garlic hit him. The soldiers wore ropes of it around their necks. He hurried through the throng of soldiers and moved through the corridors to a back entrance where he deposited his crate on the tail piece of the first cart. He took in a cleansing breath and glanced around him.

The moon had risen, but it was only a half-sliver, which would do little to help provide light on the road to the barracks. With any luck, the road would be a busy thoroughfare, given the high number of cavalrymen housed in Preston. Gerhardt and his men would be able to travel unmolested.

As for himself, the route they took, circuitous as it was, would probably take unused country lanes and be twice as long. Certainly, vampires had the advantage of them in abilities, but if they were lying in wait for Gerhardt, they would be disappointed, and they would not be able to track down the real vaccines easily.

Gerhardt came out and set his crate down in the other cart. He reached up under his capacious coat and stepped over to John.

"Here, I got you something." Gerhardt handed over a pair of iron stakes. The sight of them made John's blood run colder. He took the heavy, cool weights in his hand.

"Keep them close," Gerhardt said. "But not too close. You don't want to accidentally stake yourself."

"I'm dying of laughter." John tucked the stakes into his belt and pulled his waistcoat over them. He wiggled his fingers in Gerhardt's direction. "Did you get all your hunting equipment replaced?"

"I did." He held open one side of his coat revealing a leather harness rippling with silver stakes hung diagonally on his chest and on his waist a belt holding stoppered vials, silver bullets, and a brace of pistols.

"I take it I am going with the real vaccines?" John asked in a barely audible whisper.

Gerhardt nodded.

"Is there anyone out here other than these men?" Gerhardt whispered back and then gestured to the guards who were filing out of the house with the crates. John hadn't sensed anything unusual when he had first stepped out of the house, but he closed his eyes and reached out with his hearing and breathed in deeply through his nose. A flood of sensations erupted over him: a stagnant pond somewhere to his right and a hundred yards or so away, fresh animal droppings, one of the guardsmen who favored

147

a spiced hair oil from the orient, a squirrel rustling in its nest in the oak at the front of the house, a whispered argument between two girls as to a certain cavalryman they hoped would notice them…. The sensations continued. One by one he identified them and discarded them as unimportant.

Finally he opened his eyes and shook his head. "Nothing that might cause him alarm."

"At least we have that going for us," Gerhardt said. He sprang up into the second cart which held the red-labeled crates. The outriders took up their positions on either side, loaded down with ropes of garlic around their necks, their belts bristling with wooden stakes. More guards, similarly accoutered, sprang onto the back.

"See you on the other side," John said. Gerhardt grinned at him and tugged at his forelock. The cart rumbled away and John climbed up onto the bench of the cart he was to take. A waft of garlic from the driver's neckpiece moved towards him and John held his breath. At least once they were moving the breeze would remove the stench somewhat. The driver, a crusty old soldier whose heart beat slow and steady, chewed on the stub of an expired cheroot and watched as John leaned away from him. Beside them the outriders fell into step and the other guards found seats among the crates in the bed of the cart. The driver slapped the reins and the cart began to move into darkness that cloaked the street, its lanterns swinging and casting bobbing black shadows on the ground beside them.

"What's your name, soldier?"

"Jack Hawkins."

"Well, than, Hawkins," John, said proffering his hand, "John Grissom, at your service. I hope you are ready for a lively adventure this evening. It may came to nothing, but it may not."

Hawkins winked at him.

"High spirits, have you? Hoping for the worst?"

John smiled at him. He was, in truth, trying to work himself up for the occasion of their being attacked. It was nerve-wracking to know precisely how dangerous were the undead men they could be going up against. At their worst – or best, as it were – vampires were almost impossible to see for their fleetness, had near indomitable strength, and didn't suffer the usual weaknesses the average man was subject to. If they were lying in wait for Gerhardt, he didn't envy him the job.

"What's with the garlic?" Hawkins asked, plucking at the rope around his neck.

"Trust me, I'd rather do without it. But Crown orders." John replied. He briefly wondered whether it was possible to build an immunity to the stuff, first perhaps by starting with a constant exposure to the smell in small doses. It was worth looking into.

"Sounds like a hocus pocus superstition."

John slanted a glance over at Hawkins and shook his head noncommittally.

"It's lucky for you I was on duty this evening," Hawkins resumed.

"How's that?"

"No one else knows the area like I do. I grew up in Preston-on-Hove. When war with the French comes along, every mother in Brighton, yeoman and gentry alike, goes loose in their attic for fear of invasion. My mother was no different. She pressed my father into teaching us boys fifteen different routes through the countryside to safety." He chuckled and chucked the reins on the horses back. "Seems our good King George list'ed to those wives, for now we have a garrison and the might and strength of the Royal Army quartered here near year round."

As John had expected, the quarter moon did not provide any significant light on the country roads and lanes. Even to his bespectacled eyes, the pale, ghostly track became indiscernible 100 feet out. They moved slowly.

149

John pulled out his pocket watch wondering if they would make it to the rendezvous point in time, or if they would have the entire regiment of 10th Hussars standing about shuffling their feet.

The jingling harnesses provided incongruous merriment to the somber group. John could smell the cavalrymen's fear, almost feel the tension in the muscles as they sat or rode, their fingers resting near the triggers. They hadn't been told the specifics, but warnings of a possible attack had been enough to put them on edge. Hadn't they all heard about unexpected riots that claimed the lives of infantrymen in Dartmoor only last month?

The lights from houses in the distance winked in and out as the horses pulled them through lanes that cut between hills and over short bridges. Suddenly, one of the horses shied, pulling the cart toward a ditch on the side of the track. Snorting and pawing, the two horses struggled against each other. Hawkins sawed on the reins, trying to get them back under control. Yells erupted on all sides of them as the outriders attempted to prevent the horses from bucking, or worse, sprinting away. The nervous guards on the back clutched at the cart with one hand and their rifles with the other, not knowing what, or who, had caused the ruckus. Shouts of fear and curiosity cut through the dark. John closed his eyes, forcing himself to filter through the various sounds and smells assailing his senses, seeking further and further out for what threatened them. And then a shot rang out in the chaos.

CHAPTER 12

"What was that? Is anyone hurt?" John asked. He sniffed for the scent of blood, but smelled none. Nor did he sense anyone who hadn't already been riding with them. He did, however, smell the rabbit that had no doubt caused the commotion. "Everyone be calm. It was just a rabbit."

Hawkins snorted.

"It's blacker than a witch's soul out here, but you saw the rabbit that spooked the horses. Those be powerful spectacles, Mr. Grissom, if I do say so."

"Indeed. I would be unable to function without them," John returned. He hadn't lied. "The lanterns are helpful."

The horses were led back onto the road. Behind him the soldiers settled into their spots once more and the outriders took up their places on either side. John wrinkled his nose. The smell of their fear induced sweat and adrenaline was so strong he was near to experiencing the emotion himself. Hawkins clicked his tongue, snapped the reins, and they were moving once more.

"How much longer?" John asked.

"After the next rise, the lights from Preston will come into view."

John's teeth knocked together as the cart jerked and jostled him. He wondered if Gerhardt had made it to the parade grounds unmolested. Thinking on it was futile. He would know when he knew.

The cart trundled up the rise, and, as promised, Preston lay in the distance. Hawkins seemed surer of his approach with the village in sight. He slapped the reins and hurried the horses into a canter. They lurched down the roads, seeming to take every conceivable turn off.

"You do realize we are going to Preston, Hawkins?" John asked, when they took yet another turn.

"Orders were to take you by the most circuitous path I know. And this is it. Don't worry, sir! We'll get you there."

John clenched his jaw against the bone-jarring knocks and bumps of the cart as the horses picked up the pace. Of course, on a dirt lane, rutted and infrequently used, it was impossible for them to move faster than a quick trot for more than a few strides, but Hawkins was just skirting the line of safety on that head.

The lights grew closer and closer until John could make out the architectural details of the new massive housing blocks that hundreds of soldiers temporarily called home. The stables lay further away from them, identifiable by smell and the muted sounds of almost a thousand horses.

"We're entering town from the North," Hawkins said. "We'll be going right past the King and Queen. You might consider laying your head there tonight."

As they rolled into the sleepy village, its houses nestled next to each other and sharing gardens and yards, lights from within the homes provided a shade more illumination on their road. They turned down several lanes branching through the village and then turned onto the cobbled main road. Within minutes, a contingent of cavalrymen came riding to meet them, all of them wearing ropes of garlic around their necks. Perhaps they would make it part of the uniform, John thought. With a clatter of hooves, they drew up abreast of them, providing an escort that stretched in front and behind five deep.

"We've been watching for you, sir. Your servant, Lieutenant Sanders," an unknown red-coated rider said to John. Despite the militant and determined look in his eye, Sanders was all of twenty-one years, by John's guess, and the younger son of a lord from his accent. John hazarded the boy's chin wouldn't need scraping but twice in a twelve month. The young lieutenant proffered a hand and continued speaking, his words joining together in a rambling way, as if his thoughts were fleeing in seven different directions and he had to gather them together at once. "Glad to see you unharmed. I'm afraid your friend was not so lucky. They fell afoul of an assailant on the way in, just outside of Preston, not moments ago."

John swallowed. Not that he could claim friendship with Gerhardt, but the man's loss would be a great loss for England, given his various talents. "And?"

"Mr. Van Helsing was the only man standing when we arrived."

"How many wounded?"

"You mean dead, sir," Sanders bit out angrily. "All of them. Six guards and two outriders. I don't know how he –"

"How many?"

"Just the one assailant that I saw."

"No, how many of you were there?"

"Twenty. Major Harrison sent us to meet Van Helsing as soon as he got into Preston."

"And Van Helsing?"

"Alive. In need of a surgeon. But I don't believe it's anything a good bottle of French brandy and some stitches won't fix. Major Harrison is seeing to his care and he's a rare good saw bones."

"Did Van Helsing look particularly pale or seem unresponsive?"

The cavalryman looked around at his fellows, at a loss for an answer.

"I'm not a surgeon, Mr. Grissom. He looked like a man who had just barely survived a fight to the death. Of course, the assailant got away, but –"

"I thought you captured him!" John exclaimed sharply.

"No. He slipped away into the night with all the stealth and speed of one of those infernal bat creatures." Sanders shivered in his saddle, looking, for a moment, impossibly young. "Hate the things."

153

"Do you mean he turned into a bat?!" John asked. That would add a whole new dimension to vampiric abilities.

Hawkins leveled a glance at John.

"No need to go scaring the cub, now, Mr. Grissom," Hawkins muttered out of the side of his mouth.

"Good heavens, no!" Sanders sputtered. "Turned into a-? That's the most superstitious drivel -"

"I was just making a May game of you, Lieutenant. No need to fly up in the boughs," John assured him.

The cart drew up alongside the parade grounds. Hawkins spoke soft commands and pulled up on the reins. The cart stopped near a tent set up in the field. A group of men milled beneath it clustered together in twos and threes, their rifles slung over their shoulders. John stood up and stretched his limbs, grateful the ride was over and that they had arrived with nary a death on their hands.

He took a deep whiff of the air, but before it was expelled he realized using his senses to locate a vampire would be an exercise in futility. Waite would be smart enough to either cloak his scent, or disguise it, and with the many heartbeats around him, John wouldn't be able to tell if they were about to be attacked. If Waite attacked them again, John knew it very well could be his last chance to nab him. The vampire wouldn't put himself at such risk again.

He jumped down from the cart.

"Let's get this over with, then."

The crates were brought over to a table beneath the tent. Curious cavalrymen watched as John set up lancets. Each inoculation involved no more than a few minutes as a small wound was inflicted and then the cowpox-infected liquid was rubbed onto the wound. But a few didn't take well to voluntarily subjecting themselves.

"Come, my good man. It's no worse than a nick when you're shaving," John said to one young man who was quaking at the sight of the lancet. "It will be over within a few seconds. You needn't even watch. Probably won't realize it's already been done and over until we call for the next person."

The soldier nodded his head, thrust his arm and looked away. With professional speed, John shoved up the shirt sleeve, swabbed his forearm, nicked the skin, and wiped the wound with a liberal amount of the serum. A small cotton bandage tied around the arm finished it off.

"I see you made it!" a voice called out. John looked up to see Major Harrison approaching the brightly lit tent. John moved on to the next man as he waited for the army surgeon to come closer.

"I did, indeed," John said, when the army surgeon was close enough to speak with without shouting. "I heard Gerhardt wasn't so fortunate."

"Whoever it was that attacked left him with some nasty looking wounds. He'll have a thin scar on his face." Harrison looked over the remaining members of the regiment. "How are they taking it?"

John looked up from the soldier he was attending.

"Most grumble about the interruption to their evening. It's understandable." John paused and waited for the soldier to rise, pausing the next one in line. "I assume that you have told no one about what happened earlier this evening?"

The surgeon shook his head and gave a grim laugh. "As I told Van Helsing, I wouldn't know who to tell. No one would believe me. And if, by keeping this secret, I help protect England, you'd have to flay me alive before I spoke of it to anyone."

"And not even then, right?" John pressed, though he smiled all the same. Harrison nodded. John waved another soldier over. The major removed his coat, rolled up his sleeves, and plucked a fresh apron from the supply crate.

"Think we can get them all knocked out within the hour?" Harrison asked, hailing a soldier to come over.

"I can only hope," John said. He blinked his eyes open as wide as they could go several times. "Or I might end up nicking something important."

The soldier in front of him flinched.

"I jest, of course," John said. He grimaced apologetically at Major Harrison before applying himself to his work again.

****

John whistled.

"As if didn't think you were ugly before!" John stepped into the wedding suite of the King and Queen where Van Helsing lay almost drowning in bed sheets and pillows, one arm strapped to his chest. John and the Major had finished their inoculations at close to one in the morning. On Hawkins' recommendation, John sought out the King and Queen, the inn closest to the barracks and a well-loved spot complete with tap room and parlors. It was tempting to immediately find his bed, but it wasn't at all the thing to do so without stopping by to see how Gerhardt was faring.

"Just so, Grissom. Just so," Gerhard responded, picking at the bandage wrapped across his brow. "Waite near took my eye out."

"No significant damage, then?" John asked, sinking into a chair next to the bed.

"No. Nothing I can't recover from given a good rest."

"I brought you something. Compliments of the King's Own who will soon be feeling the joys of itching like mad and fevers brought on by cowpox serum. They thought you deserved some reward for your fearless combat alongside their fellow cavalrymen." John pulled out a flask. Gerhardt's eyes lit up as he leaned across to grab it.

He pulled the cork out with his teeth and took a whiff. The pillows deflated as he sank back against a mound of

156

bedding, a blissful smile of happiness on his battered features.

"Now, I've no interest in how this was acquired, but this is French brandy if I've ever had it." He swallowed from the flask and offered it to John, who waved it away. Gerhardt shrugged and sipped again. "So, now that you've seen the *invalid-*"

John laughed.

"Invalid?" he chortled. "You've suffered a two inch cut on your face, a dislocated left arm, a puncture wound in the right shoulder, and you're already perking up."

"Barely missed my lung."

"You'll survive. What's more, I hazard to say, you'll be knocking on my door before dawn tomorrow, raring to get back to Town."

"I will not. I'm luxuriating."

"You couldn't stay away even if you wanted to. Waite is still on the loose, and we still have to bring all this to the attention of White Hall. Enjoy the wedding suite while you can, but mark my word, I said it. You'll be knocking on my door before dawn tomorrow."

Gerhardt raked a hand through his hair and dropped his head back.

"If I weren't a Catholic, and I'm not such a good one at that, I would say, 'Damn that man.' Waite." Gerhardt lifted his eyes to the heavens, and raised a defensive hand. "I'm not saying it. But, Lord, it is very hard not to despise him."

John snorted mirthlessly. "A cure. When I get back, after we go to White Hall, while you are off trying to discover where Waite is, I am going back to my laboratory, and I am going to throw myself into discovering a cure. Just think on it. If we could administer Waite with an injection while he slept during the day, he would be powerless."

"A powerless Waite would be a beautiful thing."

"Now," John said, rising to his feet, "I'll leave you to your beauty sleep – though I fear your pretty looks are beyond repair given the scar you'll have."

"It only adds to my allure. The ladies will love it."

John paused on his way out the door. "Where's the chamber pot? I think I'm going to cast up my accounts."

John left the room, Gerhardt's laughter following him out. He entered his own room down the hall. It was, in comparison, a much more modest bedchamber. But the bed had clean sheets warmer than his own skin, so the lack of a mirror and the wrinkled linen curtains didn't make a dint on his satisfaction. He stripped down to his small clothes, dove in, and was drifting to sleep within minutes.

****

There were some things in life that spoiled a man. John heaved a sigh at the thought of the hired hacks he had been accustomed to. It wasn't as if he couldn't afford to keep a mount stabled, but he had thought since the hacks were available there wasn't much point in purchasing his own mount. Now, having used Gerhardt's racing blood to get from Town to Brighton and back again, he saw there was very much a point. Perhaps Gerhardt would consider selling one the horses. After all, what would he do with two mounts? Did he keep his own stables in Town? It appeared he would now.

The matched stallions trotted in easy tandem as they left White Hall. John sighed again. After a grueling three hour interview with Foreign Secretary Lord Wellesley, there didn't seem to be a single part of him left unearthed. His secret was officially out to the English government. Of course, he hoped the monarch would see it as the benefit it could be and use it toward his advantage. With an ability to detect forces outside of the norm, he could prove an adept addition to the Minister's secret group of Crown-sanctioned investigators.

His heart lifted more than he liked at the thought of seeing his assistant – he must keep in mind what she was – again. But he promised himself to be so busy that he shouldn't even have time for socializing or making himself available at tea time. They needed that cure if they were going to overcome Waite. The man was quick, ruthless, and a vampire of impressive talents. The garlic ropes of the guards traveling with Gerhardt had left him unfazed. And Gerhardt had not been able to stake the man for being outmaneuvered.

With an army of 'Blood gifted' vampire servants and volunteer blood slaves at his sprawling house on St. James Street they would have to have near miraculous good luck to discover Waite's place of rest during the day. Because things could never by easy, now could they? They couldn't just stumble on Waite resting in a coffin and stake him. They couldn't just torch the house, catching him between the inferno of the blaze and the sunlight which would sear his skin to ash within seconds. No, for a surety they would have to take on Waite's entire 'Order of the Blood' before they unearthed his lair.

Gerhardt pulled up. They were only a few blocks from the laboratory, but the vampire hunter would be attempting to discover more information on Waite's movements from his paid informants. He had removed his remaining bandages, leaving a thin, reddened scar tracing its way over his brow.

"You can leave Glory o' the Strand at the stables near the laboratory. Please give Miss Isherwood my compliments."

"You may stop by when you are done and give them yourself, if you like," John said, sitting back in the saddle."

"I might do that." Gerhardt nodded in John's direction and clucked his tongue at the stallion. John moved away down the street, skirting carriages and fellow riders. It was a busy day on the thoroughfare and both genteel and lower class riders and coaches jockeyed for room. A few more minutes brought him to the stables where he left his mount and continued on foot. She was probably waiting for him, even now, anxious to know the outcome. His steps hurried a bit more.

He all but leapt up the steps to the front door, but then, having gained entrance, he paused in the foyer, forcing himself to slow down. He went up the stairs slowly. The study and library was empty, as was the back room. He took himself up the stairs again to the attic rooms. The monkeys were happy to see him, as evidenced by the raucous screeching that exploded upon his entrance. But other than the test animals, there was no one to greet him.

A small wooden box, all of six inches by six inches, sat on the laboratory table, next to his microscope. Black German lettering was stenciled across its sides. John ran his hand across the lid. Wherever Miss Isherwood was, it appeared she had been at the laboratory long enough to receive a box from Waite. He slid the tip of his pen knife underneath the wooden lid and pried it up. Wrapped in puffs of wool and nestled in a bed of straw, the lens winked up at him in the afternoon light. He picked it up and turned it over in his fingers. No identifying marks indicating the craftsman. John wondered if any lives had been lost to get it. Knowing what he knew now, he couldn't believe Waite had used any fair means to acquire it. Then again, Waite had connections in Germany. Perhaps one of them was a glazier of renown.

****

The sound of someone hammering on the front door reached its way up the stairs. The quick, staccato bursts demanded urgency. John set the lens back in the box and ran down the stairs two at a time.

"Yes, what is it?" John asked as he threw open the door. A youth in well-used, mended clothing stood without, turning his hat in his hands.

"From the Flying Pheasant, in Fowlton. Miss Isherwood sent me with a message." He pulled out a folded piece of paper from stained breeches. John took it from him and unfolded it. As his eyes scanned the familiar lettering, his breath seized up. He clutched the note in one fist.

"She was at the inn, then?" John asked.

"She was."

John dug a coin out of his pocket and slapped it into the boy's hand.

"Thank you, lad. If you care to ride with me, I can return you since I will be going that way immediately."

The boy settled his hat atop his unruly curls.

"No, thank you, sir. My aunt lives in Town. I'll see her before I go."

John watched the boy walk away and then ran toward the stables. Glory' would be settled down in his stall by now, but after their leisurely return from Brighton, he could handle a quick run.

Within a half hour he was on the road to Fowlton. When he left the clusters of houses and close traffic of the city, he would give Glory' his head. With any luck, he would make it to the Pheasant in twenty minutes. He could only imagine the anxiety Miss Isherwood must be suffering while she waited for aid to arrive. Her note, short and full of splotches from haste, had requested his help after she had awakened that morning to discover her father missing. The cobbled stone street turned to hard-packed dirt. Carts and drays grew less frequent.

John touched his heels to Glory's withers and the horse shot forward. He focused on his form and kept his senses alert to his surroundings. The swish and pull of the blood as it pulsed through the stallion's great heart was reflected in the movement of his body in the saddle.

"Stand and deliver!" A rider yelled, swooping out of a copse on the side of the road to gallop behind him. The man's muffler covered his face, a ragged cape flapping behind him. But in his hand was a pistol John assumed he had every intention of using. Glory', sensing the other horses trying to nose ahead of him, took the bit and stretched out, long legs flashing into a blur. John had no doubt he could outrun them.

The rider was joined by another behind him. The two had the normal, regular heartbeats of humans. But it occurred to him that the bandits had likely strung out their men in stages to ensure that someone would catch him. John kept his eyes peeled for others. Up ahead, the road curved. As sure as he was a vampire, he knew with almost seer-like knowledge that there would be others lying in wait around that curve.

He turned Glory off the road and cut into a field. His speed slowed a fraction as Glory's hooves sank into the short, sheep-shorn grass. Shouts and yells erupted behind and to his left. The men he knew were lying in wait raced out of where they had been hidden behind an outcropping of rock. They were much closer than his first pursuers.

As if sensing his anxiety, Glory flattened his neck even further, and pinned his ears back, streaking forward without caution.

Abruptly the stallion stumbled and faltered. Then John was flying over his head and bouncing down a shallow hillside. As he tumbled, he caught glimpses of the big horse coming down the hill after him in an awkward twisting of hooves and legs and trunk. He lay on his back on the ground, his spectacles knocked askew, if still miraculously on his face, his arms and legs spread-eagled. He was almost afraid to move them because of what he might find. His breath sounded loud in his ears, coming hard and fast.

Seconds after he had flopped to a stop, his pursuers had him surrounded. There were four of them, each as muffled and disguised as the rest. They slid off their mounts.

"Pity about the stallion," one of the men grumbled. He came to a stop next to John's desperate horse. The creature was in obvious distress, making the attempt to rise and failing repeatedly.

"Aye, but we're fortunate the foxhole was so untimely. It never does to displease his lordship," another replied. The speaker pulled out a pistol and moment later a shot rang out, and then another. But for John's own ragged breathing, silence rang in the clearing.

The remaining two men grasped him under the shoulders and hauled him to his feet. Any hope of mercy John might have had from the horse sympathizer died as the man stepped forward and brought out a silver stake from the inside of his coat.

John heaved himself backward attempting to twist out of their grasp, but the two men were prepared for it. They swayed, held. The man holding the silver stake raised it for John's perusal.

"We were given orders to bring you in. And that if you gave us any objection, to deal with you as we saw fit."

John spit. Waite's blood slaves. The man standing in front of him plowed a fist into John's cheek. His spectacles went flying.

"Where's Van Helsing?" John ground out. "What did you do with him?"

The question gave the man pause, but then he launched a powerful fist into John's stomach. John gasped as he was robbed of air, and pain bloomed across his abdomen.

"No questions."

CHAPTER 13

The horses came to a stop outside the Waite mansion. John, now bound, muffled and hooded, could barely see in the dark. They had been kind enough to return his spectacles, but on a moonless night, with lit street lamps blocks away and a deep, tree-filled lawn running around the perimeter, little light from the City was cast on the house. He sensed more than saw the vampires that were stationed around the grounds and house. Their heartbeats didn't give them away, but all of them carried a particular perfume which John dubbed to himself, "Waite's House."

Rough hands pulled him down off the saddle. He fell to the ground with a grunt and then rolled to his knees.

"Grissom, you disappoint me." The words cut through the expanse of night air that lay between John and the speaker. Though John could not make out much more of him than a large, dark silhouette, Waite's voice, cold and harsh, was unmistakable.

The next moment, John only registering the movement after the fact, Waite launched a kick to the side of his head. John landed on his side, flashing lights exploding across his vision.

"Bring him in."

Two heartless creatures pulled him to his feet and dragged him up out of the gravel and into the house. John shook his head and wrinkled his nose to straighten his spectacles on his face. The muffler had saved them from flying off when Waite kicked him. He squinted in the blazing light shed by every light giving feature in the house. The entire row of chandeliers in the front hall had been lit, as well as branched candelabras on the wall every three feet. John thought it decidedly overdone.

They shoved him forward down the hall, past a staircase leading to the upper gallery, past the drawing room and dining room where he had been entertained more than a month before. He followed in the path of a vampire, who, by his attire, acted as butler – *evening butler?* John thought. The man's powerful shoulders and thick neck, coupled with the fact that Waite kept him on as the first person to greet guests, were intimidating evidence of what his probable abilities were as a vampire.

They went down a set of servant's stairs in the back of the house, filed through kitchens that were larger almost than his whole set of rooms and came to a stop outside a heavy wooden door with straps of studded iron holding it together. John didn't have a moment's doubt as to what lay on the other side.

The butler unlocked it and led the way down a narrow flight of stairs walled in with stone. The hallway leveled out again. Torches hung on the walls, flames guttering. More iron-banded doors were stationed every six feet, three on each side with sliding door slots located at eye level and on bottom. It was a regular dungeon. Though a normal human probably could not hear the noises which emanated from their interiors, the sounds were prominent in his ears.

In some, he heard sobbing, in others urgent whispers for silence so they could hear what was going on. All of the captive humans had heartbeats that beat a mile a minute. A few of the doors lay silent, but for faint rustling. *Captive vampires?* John asked himself. It appeared he wasn't going to be the only one.

The butler opened a door containing, from what John could hear, only a single human occupant. They thrust him inside and shut the door behind him before he could make out the other person in the small room.

Utter darkness cloaked the room. He smelled mold and earthy water. He turned at the sound of shifting in the corner. Then, under the earthy scent of human dirt and an unwashed body, he smelled it. Miss Isherwood's perfume.

"Miss Isherwood!" he whispered. John shook with anger. More so than he had ever wished it before, he wished he had the vampiric strength that would enable him to shed the ropes he was bound with. No matter how violently he strained against them, his arms remained pinioned behind him.

"Who - who is it?" Her voice caught with fear.

"Your favorite bacteriologist, at your service."

"What?!" she said. She scrambled toward him, and then her hands found him, blindly patting his chest and arms. "What are you doing here? Who else knows you're here? Does Gerhardt know? Will he try to rescue us?"

"As far as I know, no one knows. But Gerhardt is no fool, he will have suspected something untoward if he went to the lab this evening and no one was there and no word left for him. Now, can you feel the ropes holding me?"

She went around his back and patted at his arms again. "Yes."

"Do you think you could loosen them?"

She began working on the knots, but in the dark John knew it wouldn't be easy.

"How did you come to be here?" John asked.

"I was at the laboratory this morning when a boy stopped by saying he was from the Flying Pheasant. He told me my father had sent word that I was needed at home right away." She tugged at his wrists, but the knots seemed to hold as fast as ever. "Of course, with such an emergency, I left right away. I hailed the first hackney I saw, but when I got in, there was a man in the carriage with me. I hadn't noticed the shades were drawn on the windows. He held a pistol and told me that if I screamed, he would shoot me and dump my body in the street. They brought me here."

"Did he blindfold you?" John asked over his shoulder.

"No."

That was not good.

"And your father?"

166

"I don't know. Maybe he's perfectly well. The message was only a ruse, wasn't it?"

"I think so. I, too, received a message from a boy who claimed he was from the Flying Pheasant. Said you needed me right away."

"And you came," she breathed.

"Yes. I am not altogether without a heart."

She fell quiet for a moment as she worked on the knots.

"There's water in the corner, a bucket of it," she said. "But it might kill you if you drink it. Do you even drink water?"

"No. And it wouldn't kill me anyway." Silence fell between them for several beats, the only sound in his ears being the rapid beat of her heart.

"Do you – do you suppose they will kill us then?" Miss Isherwood asked.

"Yes."

Silence fell again, and then, "Mr. Grissom –"

"This close to death, I think we can dispense with formalities. Please, call me John."

"John, then." Her hands paused their work on his bindings. "When was the last time you fed?"

"Yesterday morning, on the way back from Brighton. Why?"

"What if nobody comes to give you blood?"

Why would they not bring him blood? They were vampires. They knew what would happen if…. John felt sick. It had not occurred to him that they were lodged together in hopes that he would subject her to just such a fate. Was Waite *such* a villain?

He turned to face her even though he couldn't see her in the dark.

"How much time do we have before you…?" She trailed off.

"At worst, tomorrow morning. At best, tomorrow night." John breathed deeply, fighting off panic. He

167

squeezed his eyes shut. This was horrible. Their situation could not get any worse. They would have to try to escape. Perhaps if a guard came back, they could-

"Should I continue attempting to untie you then?" she asked.

"We don't know if that is what they are planning."

"No. But why else would they have put us in the same cell together?"

"Lack of space?" John asked, thinking of the sounds he had heard coming from the other cells.

She smacked him on the shoulder. "You're jesting? Now? We're talking about you going raving mad and attacking me, only to drain my blood. I think I am going to be sick."

There were rustles of movement in front of him.

"Yes, you're right," John said. "Apologies. I was just trying to… diffuse my own anxiety over it. No, don't untie me."

Heaven help him! They had stuck him in a dungeon with a human. Come morning the hunger pains would start to grow in intensity until they consumed his very reason. And then, there would be nothing she could do to stop him.

"I have an idea." Her voice came from lower down, as if she was bent over, which made sense if she was feeling sick. "You aren't going to like it. *I* am not going to like it."

John waited. What could she possibly say that would change the fact that tomorrow he would attack her, no matter what degree of affection he felt for her now? He stepped across the room carefully until he found the wall. He slid down, rested his shoulders against the stones, and tipped his head back. The silence stretched between them, as if she didn't want to put voice to the idea herself.

She sighed. "I think we have to do what we can to – to give Gerhardt as much time as possible to launch a rescue."

John shook his head.

168

"What do you mean? I don't have any control over when I require…." He was revolting. His eyes watered, and he banged his head against the stones in frustration.

"We know the human body regenerates blood, right?" she asked. "You might have to feed – "

"Don't. Don't even suggest it."

"John, it might work. It will help you control the craving. If we wait to have you do this until you are insane with hunger, you will take too much at one time – and then I'll die."

"What if you contract," John paused and swallowed. He tried again, "What if you contract my affliction? There is no going back from that."

"Not yet, no. You *are* working on a cure, though. And what do we even know about how it is contracted? Is it from a single bite? From an exchange of blood? From the saliva? Or is it only contracted after the body has been made sufficiently vulnerable from lack of blood? We don't know the answers to those questions, but we do know what will happen if we allow you to reach the point where you lose your reason. Do you not see?"

John dropped his head to his drawn up knees. He wasn't a cannibal, and there was something so repellant at the thought of sustaining his own life through consuming hers. And if he did this, what if he could never go back to the blood of irrational animals? Would animals be enough? Or would it so affect his vampiric side that his body would demand human – he shivered, cutting off the thought.

"I- I can't. I'm sorry."

He heard rustling and then angry footsteps approached. She settled down in front of him.

"You listen to me, John Grissom, if you think I am going to die a horrific death because your sense of delicacy prevents your feeding off me in small amounts, you have got another think coming." She patted at him until she felt his face, and then stabbed him in the chest with a finger.

"You are going to do it. In regular intervals. Small amounts. We have water, so at least I'll be able to replenish my liquids. You do it, or...."

"Or what?"

"Or I'll probably go to hell for hating you as you kill me."

"You say this now, but when it comes down to it – will I be forgiven?"

"John, you aren't doing this because you want to. I know that. God knows that. And you won't be killing me by doing it."

"What if Gerhardt never rescues us, and we run out of water, and they just leave us in here?" John sighed. "Never mind. I suppose I am just being stupid. We'll cross that bridge when we come to it, won't we."

"Yes." She paused and then rested a hand on his knee. "I'm sorry. I know the thought of it disgusts you."

John swallowed.

"I don't know," John said. "Sometimes I think, what if I don't do it because I am afraid I will really enjoy it? What if my disgust isn't so much for the act itself, but for the possibility that I might receive some sort of satisfaction from it? What kind of a person does that make me?"

Miss Isherwood didn't answer.

"I think..." she said finally. "I think it makes you human. Those fears are a good thing. There is no sin we are incapable of committing. Without those fears, God's laws, and our immortal soul, we are no better than mindless animals."

"Do you really believe that?"

"Of course. Don't you?"

John nodded. He did. Intellectually, in his head, he did. But that didn't prevent him from revolting against the idea of feeding off her. Nevertheless, at this point, she was right. He had an obligation to do whatever he could to prevent himself from losing his mind and killing her.

"I'll do it," he said quickly. If he didn't get the words out in time, he would have time to doubt, to change his mind. "Don't ask me if I'm sure, because I'm not."

"Wasn't planning on it." She moved back across the room. "So, when should we, er, attempt the first one?"

John shrugged in the dark. He was going to have to work himself up to it. "At dawn, when my appetite is just beginning to rear its ugly head."

They both sat down across the room from each other. After a time, her heartbeat slowed to a steady pumping. It soothed his spirits.

****

John stomped his feet to get his sluggish blood moving again in his limbs. He shifted his hands behind his back. He was losing feeling in his fingers from the ropes, and leaning against them hadn't helped. No one had visited them through the hours they had been waiting. He had hoped his and Henrietta's suspicions were wrong, that there was some other reason for putting him in the same cell as her.

But, intentional or not, if he did not feed soon, his hunger would become ravenous. Already he could feel the few seconds of nausea that would stretch into minutes, the precursor of pains that would become intense and fill every cell of his body until he went mad with it unless it were tended to.

"Are you ready then?" she asked. Her voice was low and quiet. She must be afraid, too, of the outcome.

"No. But we have to do it now anyway."

She rose to her feet and came toward him. Against his will, his vampiric senses took over and, as if it was particularly attuned to the sound of a heart, the sound of it filled his ears. Every motion of the muscle, each chamber filling and pushing the blood out with a throb and a swish of sound took up every space in his head. He drew deep breaths in through his nose and out through his mouth. He could feel his fingers trembling, so he clenched them into fists. The ropes cut into his wrists more because of it, but the pain helped to focus him on her, her humanity, rather than her heart.

"What do you want me to do?" she asked.

"Figure out a way to brace your hand."

"You are going to… feed, off my wrist? Will it hurt?"

"I don't know."

"But, I don't understand. Didn't you feel it when you were turned?"

"No." The silence stretched as if she was expecting more. "I can't talk about it, Miss Isherwood."

She gave a soft laugh.

"What happened to foregoing formalities? 'I think we can dispense with formalities' if you are going to gain your sustenance from me. You must call me Henrietta."

She moved away from him and slid down the wall. Rustling sounds indicated she was preparing herself.

"Ready."

John unerringly followed the sound of her heart to where she sat. He knelt before her, sickened, and at the same time seeing the necessity of what they – he – was about to do. She felt for his face with her free hand. The cool, smooth pads of her fingers against his skin felt unsettlingly intimate in the dark. She guided his face until his nose bumped into her arm.

"Wait," John said. Her hand dropped. "Would you be so kind as to remove my spectacles?"

Her fingers felt at his face again and then they were removed. Her hand came back to his cheek. She cleared her throat.

"I'm afraid."

"Yes. I know. I'm sorry."

One of her fingers approached the corner of his mouth.

"Can I feel, before you – I would just like to know what I am getting into."

John bit back a groan.

"I would rather you didn't." She would never see him the same way again if she did. Perhaps she wouldn't anyway. "But if you must…."

"I know it might make you uncomfortable, but I just… I don't like not knowing what to be prepared for."

John nodded. He dragged air into his lungs and then allowed his fangs to partially extend, edging them over his lip, slowly. He felt pressure against the one closest to her hand. When he thought she had accustomed herself to it somewhat, he extended it fully in fractions of inches. She gasped nonetheless.

"I'm sorry," John said, pulling away. "If you have any doubts –"

"No, of course not." Her fingers felt for his face again and she guided his head again to her wrist. "Now I know."

"Yes," he whispered against her skin.

John opened his mouth.

"I hope someday you will trust me enough to tell me what happened to you," she said.

John didn't respond but set his fangs against the soft skin of her wrist and pierced through.

CHAPTER 14

Under his closed eyelids the memories of her streamed over and through him. But unlike vivid pictures, or experiences, they were impressions, almost emotional but not quite that either. It was as if he had discovered her essence and it was soft, giving, and emanated a golden-pinkish glow. He might not know her particular sins or virtues, but he *knew* her, as he had never known another.

It gave him a feeling of incredible power, as if in the knowing, there was control over another being too. No wonder vampires who regularly fed on other humans felt that those incapable of experiencing such power were lesser creatures.

But the rational side of John that yet remained told him the feeling was nothing more than an illusion, a temptation. He could feel, too, the urge to drag her blood in deeply, to let it fill every part of him.

As he had feared, animal blood paled in comparison. He refused to desire more of this human flow though, fighting with everything in him that dark voice that took satisfaction in what it did for him. That temptation to sate himself of her, to take everything he could, as much as he desired, as much as she had to give.

He broke away from her, panting. His fangs receded and he sagged back to sit on his heels, weak, and at the same time stronger than he had ever felt before. She sat with her head against the wall, staring over his shoulder, blood evident on her lip where she had bit it. Had she been biting her lip against pain he had caused her? Her hand lay in her lap, two small puncture wounds oozing a thin trickle of blood. Without thinking about it he pulled violently on his restraints, frustrated at his inability to take her hand. The ropes snagged on his wrists, and then gave.

He held his hands out in front of him, realizing that he could see them, and in perfect detail. Henrietta roused, pawed at the edge of her skirts and began ripping a length off the bottom of her petticoat. He reached out and stilled her hands. Without a word he took out his handkerchief and dabbed the blood of her wrist.

"Did it hurt?" he asked in a whisper.

"No. Yes. Not physically."

He removed his cravat, tore a section off and tied it around her wrist. They would need more bandages later.

"It was more like, an invasion," she continued. She drew in a steadying breath and clasped her injured wrist. "Like I couldn't keep you out. Did you – what did you see?"

John didn't answer right away. How could he possibly put into words what he had experienced?

"You," he finally said. "I saw you."

She closed her eyes.

"Henrietta."

She opened her eyes again, blindly staring in his direction.

"Are you feeling ill? Faint?"

"No. But I am sitting. Maybe if I were standing I would be."

"Let's not try it."

John looked about the cell. It was bare of all but the bucket of water in the corner, and another bucket on the other side for personal business. She hadn't had need to make use of it in his presence yet, and he wouldn't ever have to. He hated knowing how humiliating this night would be to her. Such intimacy was the province of married folk and they were far from that.

"John."

He turned back to her to find her staring at him intently.

"Yes?"

"Your eyes."

175

John lifted a hand to his eyes and then paused.

"Good heavens! Your hands, John. They're free. When did that happen?" She grabbed at him wildly and then found his arms. Her fingers felt for the ropes. "Where did they go? How did you get free? Those knots were impossible."

"Apparently the heightened vampiric abilities are due to their feeding off human blood. A conclusion I never would have arrived at had I not been obliged to take part in this experiment."

"Do be quiet, John." She leaned forward more and held his face in her hands. He ceased breathing. "Have you seen their eyes in the dark?"

"Full dark? Yes. Why?"

Her gaze carefully studied one of his eyes, and then the other.

"It is as if your eyes have sparks of light flickering in them. And the pupils are widely dilated, the whites turn red."

John tore his face out of her grasp and jumped to his feet.

"I must appear a perfect monster!"

She said nothing, but rustling sounds told him she had risen to her feet. He turned back to her, afraid to have it confirmed, but wanting to know how low he had dropped in her estimation.

"I won't deny that it is not a sight I am accustomed to seeing. But it doesn't change who you are." She reached a hand out in his direction. "You are not a monster. I have never thought so. And I still don't. You did what you had to do in order to prevent something worse. And my body will regenerate blood."

John paced the length of the room.

"Henrietta. There's one more thing I haven't told you about, about what I saw of you, in you – however you want to phrase it."

"Yes?"

"I could see all your ailments."

She said nothing but hugged herself protectively.

"Why didn't you tell me?" he asked.

She shook her head.

"Are you taking any treatments for it?" he asked.

She laughed bitterly. "You know as well as I do none of the treatments work. Everyone who has consumption dies."

"Yes, but-"

"But what, John?" she snapped and dropped her arms. "Am I supposed to throw every remedy at it and just hope something sticks? They don't work, John. I would just rather be happy for however much time I have left."

Her lungs were just starting to deteriorate. He couldn't know the rate of the progression, but if he had to guess, she would have several more good years ahead of her. If she were careful with herself, possibly as much as ten.

"Did you want to know how much time you have?" John asked.

She shook her head immediately. "No. I don't. I just want to do what God wants me to do. And to live, to really live, and love what I am doing. I want to spend time with my father, and help you change the world, John."

John clenched his jaw at the rush of sorrow and compassion he felt for her.

"And so you shall," he said.

****

"I don't think it's going to budge."

"No," John sputtered, his muscles straining against the implacable iron-bound door that locked them in. He released a gasp of air and collapsed against the door, sliding his fingers out of the crack along the top "It'll work. I just need to loosen it up."

177

"John. It's not going to work. These doors are made to keep vampires in, I'm sure. We are in a vampire dungeon. Vampires. It wouldn't be a very good dungeon if they could just get out."

John turned to her.

"I don't think I am ever going to get used to your eyes like that," she said. "They're so… unearthly."

"Is that bad? What am I saying? Of course it is bad." John sighed and raked a hand through his hair.

Her lips skewed to the side in half-hearted agreement.

"It isn't unattractive," she said, placating his ego.

John's eyebrows shot up, but thankfully, she couldn't see him in the dark. He studied the door again. There had to be a way to get out. It wasn't possible that he finally had vampiric strength and he was locked in a cell unable to use it for anything good. He had had to subject her to another feeding after several hours since the feedings were, at best, the equivalent of tea table refreshments.

"Stand back, Henrietta. And maybe huddle up in a corner," John said. He waited until she was crouched in a corner, her hands clasped over her head.

"Whatever you're doing, John, are you sure it's a good idea?" she asked in a small voice.

"Not really, no," John said, before he took a running leap and kicked at the door. The door shook. Dust drifted down from the ceiling. The sound of it reverberated around them. The strength of his kick had thrown him back onto the floor. He groaned and held his leg. The impact had been strong enough to shatter bone, but with his new improved vampiric skeletal structure, the bones had absorbed the impact and knit together immediately. But it hurt like bones knitting together instantly, without the advantage of time.

He looked up to find Henrietta standing near him, trying to wipe a smile off her face.

178

"You were saying?" she finally said when she could speak without laughing. He collapsed onto the floor. This was not working.

Muted thumping noises sounded from above.

"Did you hear that?" he asked.

"No. What – "

"Shhh." Shouts interspersed the noises. Hope rose in him. Was it possible? "Something is going on up there."

"What time is it, do you think?"

John pulled out his watch. "Around noon."

"That is so strange that you can see it in the dark."

John laid his ear against the door. Muffled sounds of violence continued to sound above them.

"I can hear something now, but barely," Henrietta said. "Do you think the other people in the dungeons hear it too?"

"Likely. If they are vampires, they are probably accustomed to sleeping during the day so they might not be listening. But if they are, they can hear as much, if not more, than I can."

A door banged. The sound of someone running filled the corridor. "John? Miss Isherwood?"

"In here!" John shouted and began pounding on the door. "In here!"

There was a scrape of keys in a lock and then the door was opened.

"Oh, thank heavens," Henrietta breathed. Gerhardt stood in the doorway, sword in hand, and wearing his full complement of vampire-fighting gear, sans some of the stakes.

"Miss Isherwood, have you been closeted with this brute all night?"

"No need to be so horrified, Mr. Van Helsing. It wasn't by choice," she said as she crossed the threshold.

"I am scandalized. Should word get out of it, your reputation will be ruined."

She paused on the stairs and turned back to them. Her eyes met John's.

"It doesn't matter. I'm not getting married anyway. And I haven't any female friends that would throw me over."

Gerhardt looked up at John in front of him on the stairs. John shrugged his shoulders and continued following Henrietta out of the underground prison.

"How did you find us?" John asked.

"I stopped by the lab and discovered you weren't there. Singular, since you had said you would be working tonight. And then I noticed the box."

"What about it?"

"It was your beloved microscope lens, was it not?"

"Yes."

"The lid was put on askew."

John glanced at him over his shoulder.

"And?"

"And you are a meticulous, careful person. If you couldn't bother to replace the lid on it correctly, it shows you were in a hurry. Then I discovered the note from Miss Isherwood. I traced you as far as ----------- Rd. where you went off into the field, and then I knew. I gathered up my men and came right away."

They filed into the kitchen. The sunlight streaming in through the curtain-less windows set high on the wall burned his eyes and they watered. He blinked them rapidly.

"Did they find Waite?" John asked.

"No."

"No?" John repeated, rubbing at his wrist which had begun to tingle. "He must be here somewhere."

"John!" Henrietta said. She shoved his hand in his face. The back of it was red and blistered. "Get out of here, go back down stairs. I was wondering why you were looking flushed."

Gerhardt frowned at him.

"You burn in the sun?" he asked. "Since when?"

John backed into the darkened shadows of the landing leading to the prison stairs. The dim cool shade was like a salve on his skin, which began to recover and heal as soon as he was sufficiently out of the light.

"How are we going to get him home?" Henrietta asked.

"Draw the shades on the carriage. My cape can protect him when he goes out."

"Will it?" Henrietta asked, one eye on the back of his wrist which was slowly returning to its normal hue.

"Not for long, but yes. I would say just stay here, John, but I don't think it prudent to keep you in the house of the enemy."

"No. Not when we don't know where he is," John said.

"I need to round up my men and discover what they've found." Gerhardt turned to leave the kitchen for the main parts of the house. He paused and turned back to them. "You are going to have to tell me what brought on this sudden change. And if it is something we should expect from here on out."

John nodded and then added a shrug. He had no idea if his additional strength and speed were permanent. He posited that they were dependent on his maintaining himself on a regular supply of human blood, something he wasn't about to do.

Gerhardt left them.

"I am so thirsty," Henrietta said. She gulped down several cups full of water and then offered the pitcher to him. He arched a brow at her. She turned her back to him and took advantage of the water to refresh her face and finger comb her hair into some sort of order. He tried not to watch, but there was something incredibly alluring, and more intimate even than their time in the dungeon, in witnessing her make-shift toilette. Her curls sprang free regardless of her efforts to confine them. What concerned him most, however, was that she looked exhausted – as one might who spent a sleepless night confined in a dungeon with a vampire. Not to mention his required feedings.

"You should wash your wounds," John reminded her. Afraid that he would overtax a specific area, the last time he had fed, he had fed off her other arm. Now both wrists sported makeshift bandages from his cravat.

She came toward him in the recess and held out here wrists. "Untie them, if you will. I don't want to ruin the knots and have to struggle to get out of them."

John removed the cravat pieces and held her wrists in his hands. She, too, studied the puncture wounds, it being the first time she saw them in the light. The holes were about as large as the head of a pencil. They had ceased to ooze blood or liquid, and two dark gel like patches covered the holes. She looked up at him.

"Will they scar?"

John nodded.

"Where are yours?"

He had never shown them to anyone. It was evidence of a moment in his life that he desperately never wanted to remember. But he owed her that, at least. He pulled aside the collar of his shirt where, at the base of his neck, twin puncture scars were visible as raised, bone colored bumps. After a moment, he covered them again.

She pursed her lips.

"Someday, you are going to tell me," she said.

She moved away from him and went to the wash basin to bathe her wrists. Moments after John had bound them up again in clean sections of his cravat, Gerhardt returned followed by five men. Each of the men were equipped in as menacing a fashion as Gerhardt. Each of them wore several ropes of garlic around their neck. It created a cloud of stench that almost forced him backward. Despite himself, his fangs extended and he hissed. One of the men drew a crossbow up to his shoulder in alarm.

"Don't!" Gerhardt yelled, but the bolt was already zipping through the air. John instinctively threw himself to the floor, but he was too slow and it slammed through his forearm and bounced off the wall behind him. Pain bloomed in his arm as his body began immediately healing the wound. John gasped and gritted his teeth.

"John." Henrietta ran over to his side and crouched beside him. "Are you okay?"

"Well, I haven't crumbled to dust yet, so there is that," John said with a grunt. He sat up. "I'm fine."

He looked over at the men. Gerhardt had them grouped together and was attempting to explain the situation. The men looked at him curiously.

"Is that what happens?" Henrietta asked. He noticed her eyes. They seemed so concerned. Or perhaps it was merely that the dark rings beneath the near translucent fair skin made her appear more fragile than she was.

"When what happens?" he asked.

"When a vampire is staked? They turn into dust?"

John nodded and rose to his feet. "It isn't pretty."

"You didn't seem as affected by garlic before."

"No, but I should have known to expect it, given my new heightened sensitivity to sunlight."

"We'll have to do something about the laboratory."

John groaned. He hadn't even thought about it, but in order for him to use the microscope he needed extremely bright light, and that simply wasn't attainable without the sun. How would he be able to finish his work if this was permanent?

"Perhaps we could lay boards across the glass on the outside?" Henrietta continued.

Gerhardt approached with the men.

"Miss Isherwood, John. I would like to introduce you to the men I am training. They are a secret force employed by the crown to aid me, now us, in our work – you might equate them to Bow Street: Odd Crimes Division. If we are investigators, they would be along the lines of a constable."

"I would say it was a pleasure, but you shot at me," John said, waving his arm at the group.

"Apologies, sir," the culprit said. "I just reacted to the, uh, teeth."

"Just be sure whoever you're shooting at is a threat next time, if you would," John said.

"Waite isn't here," Gerhardt resumed. "We found a secret passageway that tunneled over into the next street. He's gone. But we rounded up his blood slaves, and his little army of vampires is mostly dead – or at least the ones he had here. If you catch them sleeping, it makes it easy. The slave's will be taken down to White Hall for questioning. But first, we'll need to get you home. It turns out Waite has an enclosed carriage and, even better, the carriage house is attached to the back of the house. There's no need for you to risk yourself."

John gave a sigh of relief. Not that he had been afraid, or at least, he hadn't allowed himself to think of it too much, but the pressure of knowing he would have to expose himself had been there regardless. He had seen first-hand what could happen to a "healthy" vampire who allowed the sunlight to hit his skin. He was fairly sure only a leather blanket would prevent him from blistering to dust if he went outside. For now, anyway.

"If I'm not going to die en route to the carriage, I can see myself and Henri- Miss Isherwood home," John said. "I know you have much to do before you can seek your bed."

"As you wish," Gerhardt said, although from his questioning glance it was obvious he had caught John's slip of the tongue.

****

The carriage rocked as John stepped inside. Henrietta had been waiting several moments while John attempted to cover every inch of exposed skin that he could. In the end, he had accepted the loan of Gerhardt's cape after all. With a pair of riding gloves on his hands, a high collar, and a hat pulled down low over his face, it was the best he could do to shade himself. Surely the few seconds of exposure after he stepped out would not be enough to incinerate him.

"Aren't you warm in all that clothing?" Henrietta asked after he had settled back unscathed against the squabs. The carriage suddenly darkened as the iron-sheeted window coverings were locked in place. "It's pitch black in here."

"Is it?" John asked. He could see her almost perfectly, but for her colors being slightly distorted.

"The only thing I can see is the flickering lights behind your eyes. Makes me think you're a floating head."

In the dark, John watched as her face made a grimace of disgust.

"Just wait until my teeth start glowing," John said.

Her mouth dropped in surprise, but then John started laughing. The carriage began to roll forward.

"I hope you don't mind," John said. "I asked the driver – it's one of Gerhardt's men – to take us down to the laboratory first. I'd like to pick up my notes on the serum and review them before I resume working on it."

"But I thought you wouldn't be able to," Henrietta said.

"I may not be able to look at its properties through the microscope, but there are other tests I might be able to perform. I feel like I've been away from it too long."

"Aye, you have. Gallivanting all over the countryside on race horses, getting attacked. You've no doubt forgotten everything after all that excitement. Are you sure the draw of it hasn't captured you? Think you can go back to the humble and unexciting life of research?"

"Research will always be my first love, but," John sighed, recalling his conversation with Gerhardt's employer, "should the crown call upon me to go into service, I shall do my duty without regret."

"And myself?"

"Oh, I would still expect you to maintain yourself as my research assistant. Of course, any conclusions you arrive at, you are free to seek publication on so long as you do so with due discretion." John cleared his throat and steepled his fingers above his chest. "I hope I don't offend you in some way by how I say this, but in the event that you decide to publish, you may find yourself facing certain male... prejudices against women writing on science matters. It may be to your advantage to allow me to seek publication for you, and to publish under a pen name. It is sad that we are at such a pass, but unfortunately, I have a hard time imagining the publishers I know being open to accepting a manuscript from you."

"Simply because I am female?" she asked, shaking her head in the dark.

"Yes."

She nodded and then leaned her head back against the black leather squabs. "I should have realized. It's not like I didn't know that sort of prejudice exists. I am accustomed to my father who has ever assumed my intelligence, sensibilities, and character were capable of understanding medical concepts. Perhaps a pen name would be appropriate."

"You have only to say the word and I am at your service, Miss Isherwood."

"Oh, is it Miss Isherwood now? Now that we aren't about to die? Now that you aren't in imminent danger of killing me?"

"It is." He needed to distance himself from her. There were so many things working against his inclination to pursue the friendship. And he didn't want to give people the wrong impression by slipping her given name out, as he had done with Gerhardt.

186

CHAPTER 15

Something was wrong. He knew it as soon as he stepped into the house, like one notices a bad smell in a room after coming in from outdoors. Nothing appeared to be out of place in the front rooms, but, as he stood and listened, Miss Isherwood at his shoulder, he realized it was the absence of sound that was so unsettling. Even three floors down from the laboratory he should expect to hear the noises of the animals. But silence met his ears.

"Are you entering?" Miss Isherwood asked.

"Someone has been here."

"Gerhardt mentioned he had stopped by before he found us."

"No. Follow me. And try not to make noise."

John took a moment to pick up a poker from the hearth and then slipped his shoes off. He crept toward his study door, his poker at the ready, ears straining to hear the slightest movement or beating heart in the room. Dim light filtered into the room between cracks in the curtains. He stopped at the sight that met his eyes. Almost every volume from his library had been torn down. Papers and books were strewn about the room. His desk had been demolished with an instrument of some sort, its drawers lying in broken pieces near the skeleton of the desk.

Miss Isherwood gasped and covered her mouth with a hand.

"Waite?"

John nodded. He dropped the poker to his side. "I don't have any other enemies that I know of."

"What do you think he was looking for?"

"His men were likely looking for the serum and anything I wrote about it."

"And did they find it?"

"Let's find out." He strode over to the bookshelf and began pulling it away from the wall. Pausing, he turned to Miss Isherwood. "I hate to ask, but I need to hear you say it. May I trust that after the perils we have endured, you will not betray me?"

Her mouth dropped open in surprise. Or perhaps she was offended? "Yes. Absolutely."

John nodded and pulled the bookshelf away completely. A black cast-iron door was fitted into the wall. He went over to the skeletal remains of the desk and reached up underneath the middle piece. He released a catch and a slim compartment, invisible to one not looking for it, hinged down and out from beneath the decorative front. He retrieved a key and inserted it into the door. On the other side sat a lockbox.

He glanced behind him at Miss Isherwood. He suspected she might be watching him in amazement and was not disappointed. "As a vampire, I have come not to leave anything to chance."

"What else is in there?" she asked.

"Nothing of much importance," he said, unlocking the box. He heard Miss Isherwood creep forward behind him. "Several manuscripts which, thinking on it now, don't merit such precautions."

He lifted up a stack of portfolios and set them aside. A second later he pulled out the small wooden box he had been seeking. He held it up for her to see.

"Is it in there?" Miss Isherwood asked.

John cracked the lid and then sat back on his heels, tension releasing from him. "Yes. It's here."

He flipped through several of the portfolios and came to a stop on one. "My notes, too."

The excitement over, Miss Isherwood wandered about the room.

"What a disaster. All that work, for nothing."

"It will be worse upstairs."

She turned to look at him. "Why?"

"The animals are silent."

A twinge of pain crossed her features. "Oh no. Just when Evil Monkey and I were starting to get on good terms. I will go check on them –"

John held up a hand and rose to his feet.

"I wish I could say I'll do it for you, but unfortunately the brightly lit laboratory isn't conducive to my new skin sensitivities. You know I don't care for you to see that kind of slaughter," he said. And then added, "Not that I believe you incapable of withstanding the sight of what a vampire – or vampires – can do. But if I could spare it of you, I would."

"Don't be so bacon brained, John Grissom. You may save your chivalry for one who stands in need. Do you think I would let you leave me down here in this wreck of a room, waiting for you to return – headless, likely?"

"Headless?!"

"Yes. What if they are still here? What if, somehow, they are lying in wait for you to return, knowing you would return to the laboratory soon? After all, they would not realize you have acquired an allergy to sunlight. You must admit, that's not out of the realm of possibility. And while I am fond of you, Mr. Grissom, I don't think I could quite withstand that. I'd much rather go down putting up a good fight."

"I'll walk you to the door at least. Here," he handed her the poker. "If something comes at you, just stab."

"Stay out of the light."

****

"The daylight is almost gone, Mr. Grissom." Her voice came to him further away. "You might be able to – "

Rushing steps sounded in the room. John peeked his head around the door, but immediately withdrew it as his eyes began burning. His quick glimpse had revealed Miss Isherwood at the rear of the room. She stood among a wreckage of broken glass, and jumbled cages, one arm wrapped around her waist, the other fisted in her mouth.

"Miss Isherwood, are you well?" he called out. "Or are you in need of a rescue? I will admit to hoping for the former. "

The sound of her footsteps moving toward him provided him with an answer.

"You were right," she said, popping her head out around the door frame, lips pursed in a moue of disappointment. "They were slaughtered. Blood everywhere. The laboratory is destroyed. Your microscope too."

John fingers clenched around the box and portfolio in his hands. Without a microscope he could hardly isolate the component in the serum. It would take another six months before he could acquire a new one. Another six months before he could begin to look into discovering a cure for Miss Isherwood. But who knew how long that would take, if it was possible at all?

"Does your father have a microscope?"

"No. My father just worked his practice." She bit her lip in thought. "But someone in the Medico society might have one they aren't using daily."

John nodded. "Well, there's nothing to be done now. I told the coachman to pick us up around nightfall, so if you will wait until evening, only a few hours from now I will escort you home."

"Yes. In the meantime, perhaps I can work on cleaning up this place."

"This place can wait. I think we should talk about it."

She looked over at him, her brow furrowed.

"About what? How I am going to clean? Usual method. Dust bin. Broom. Mop."

"No. You must know of what I am speaking."

190

He gave a pointed look at her wrists.

"Oh. *That* 'it.' Must we? Couldn't we just pretend – I don't know…"

"That it never happened?" John leaned back against the wall. "No. I couldn't. Do you really think you could? I'm of the opinion that it will come back to haunt you, or perhaps your dreams."

"It might that anyway." She slapped her hands against her skirts. "All right. But I'm not doing this without breaking into that lovely tea you brought me. I know you won't care for a cup, but I-"

"Allow me to make it for you. It's the least I could do. And it's been so long since I've even had the desire to."

"If you insist," she said, heading the down the stairs.

****

John sat the tea tray down in his small drawing room. He saw that Henrietta – no, Miss Isherwood, had used the time while he was making tea to straighten the room and start a fire. It wasn't much in the way of comfort. But since all they were in need of was two comfortable chairs and a small table, it served the purpose.

The tea sent up curls of perfumed steam, which, to his surprise, he enjoyed. Miss Isherwood leaned over the tray, a look of deep seated pleasure visible on her face as she breathed in deeply.

"Mmmm. Where did the biscuits come from?" she asked. She poured herself a cup and snagged a biscuit before settling back in her chair.

"I found an ancient tin in one of the cupboards in the kitchen. So I warn you, they might be inedible."

Miss Isherwood took a bite, daring him to naysay her. Her eyes rolled in her head. "This is ridiculously good for being an ancient biscuit."

191

John poured himself a cup of tea, feeling like he was reliving a memory of better times in the doing of it.

"What are you doing?" she asked. "I thought you couldn't drink it."

"Oh, I can," John said, settling back. "But it's much more pleasurable to sit here holding a warm cup and smell the aroma."

"You're an odd one, Mr. Grissom."

He inclined his head in agreement. Silence fell between them. He didn't have any idea what she might be thinking, but he couldn't help but wonder how to broach the topic. He knew it was something they needed to discuss – perhaps for his sake as much as hers.

"Do you think –" he began.

"Is it possible –" she said, in the same instance.

"You first," John said.

She set her teacup down on the table and threaded her fingers together in her lap.

"Is it possible I will turn into a vampire because of the – what do you call it, what you did?"

"To be honest, I don't know. To both questions. I don't know because I never went out of my way to familiarize myself with other vampires. I was a vampire of a different breed and never felt the need to educate myself beyond my own needs. I think we will have to wait and see."

"Well. I can't very well keep calling it 'the Episode,' or 'that thing that happened in the dungeon.'"

"Now we are talking about how we are going to talk about it... without actually talking about it."

She shot him a scathing look.

"But I take your point," he acquiesced. "When I was a younger man, I served as a medico in the army before my entry into St. Bart's to complete my studies –"

"Gracious. The army too?"

He nodded. "There was no good way to aid a man in the field. If he was wounded, his own men might carry him

192

off if he was lucky. If not, he was left there until after the battle. His life could go either way within those hours, wondering, waiting, in extreme pain, exhausted and fatigued. So many times, I thought, if only we could get to them in time. And too, there was so little I knew of surgical procedure as compared to what I know now. If I could turn back the clock... but I digress.

There was one young soldier who was brought in. He had been gut shot. But he couldn't seem to drink enough water. He was incredibly polite in the asking though. And grateful – as if we had given him the very best thing in the world in a cup of water. His name was Charlie.

Eventually, he died, but every time after that, whenever we had someone who was wanting water like that, we would raise a glass for Charlie." John paused. He lifted his tea cup in a silent salute to the soul of Charlie. "I thought perhaps, since I was, so to speak, 'Charlied,' we might go with that."

Charlie's face swam before his gaze again. The fair hair clinging against the damp forehead. His pale blue eyes. The boy hadn't yet lost that innocence of youth. He had manfully clamped down tight against the pain that burned in his abdomen, even during the surgery when they had, unsuccessfully, attempted to remove the bullet.

"Mr. Grissom," Miss Isherwood said softly. "I would be most pleased if we could name that – whatever you did – after him."

John reached for her teacup. "Now that I've sufficiently dulled you with my maudlin thoughts, I think it's time for a second cup."

He poured and handed it to her again. They both settled back into the chairs. He was unwilling to break the silence, because he didn't know how much he wanted her to know. Mainly because he didn't know how much she wanted him to know. It was decidedly uncomfortable.

"Do you think you'll ever do it again?" she asked.

Would he? He couldn't imagine experiencing that with just anybody. It was too intimate. Too close. With her, yes, if it was absolutely necessary. But he couldn't very well say that.

"Mm, no."

"Even if you had to?"

"Yes."

"Were you ever –" she swallowed, "ever tempted to take it too far?"

It would relieve her to hear a 'no' answer. She would feel so much more secure being around him. But that would be a lie. Each time he had fed from her the temptation to take as much as possible lay like a trap spread deep and wide before him.

"Yes," he answered. Her countenance fell. "But that temptation was tempered by the fact that I had the constant knowledge that your life was in my hands." He paused. "That is partially what made it so terrifying and…."

"And?"

"And I think –" he shook his head, "You may not understand this. And I don't want to scare you. I think, against my will, I found it pleasurable. I didn't desire to find it pleasurable. Not to my body, but… to my mind? I don't know if I can relate what I mean in a way you can understand. There was a sort of melding, there. Surely you felt it?"

She nodded.

"And did it please you?"

She wriggled in her chair as if the topic discomfited her.

"I won't press you on it," John said. "But if there was, it would explain some people's willingness to become blood slaves. For me, it was empowering and fearful. I was disgusted with myself, but some dark part of me was… oh, I don't know." He shook his head again.

"Enthralled?"

John looked over at her. Was she conjecturing as to his feelings, or forwarding her own?

"Yes. Exactly so," he said. "Does that scare you? My concern is that you will fear to be around me. Perhaps not now. Perhaps that fear will grow on you each time you remember being 'Charlied.'"

She shook her head and set her empty teacup down on the tray.

"No, I don't think so," she said, sinking back into the chair. "I saw too much of who you are for that. I suspect I saw as much of you, as you saw of me. But in a different way."

"Then I may assume what you saw was good. Then again, maybe you only saw what you wanted to see. Maybe you only saw what *I* wanted you to see."

"I don't know. All I know is that I believe what I saw. It aligns with what I knew about you before. That you are a man of honor, dedication, tenacity –"

"Come, Miss Isherwood, you will put me to the blush."

She scoffed at him.

"You couldn't if you tried, bloodless creature that you are." She leaned her head against one of the wings of the chair.

"You must be exhausted."

"Yes. Aren't you?"

"Not yet." He grimaced and extended his fangs a touch. "Vampire. And my hours are all off."

She yawned and opened her eyes wide in an endeavor to keep herself awake. The wafer-thin skin beneath them looked bruised.

"You know, this chair is so comfortable, I might be in danger of falling asleep." She blinked. "Oh, dear. Did I say that out loud?"

"You did. But that's all right. I will simply carry you into the carriage."

"You wouldn't."

"Don't you think I could? You would be inside before you even woke up."

"Mmm, I think I would notice," she murmured even as her heavy eyelids began to sink.

"I suppose that means we are done talking about this?"

"Hmmm...."

"Miss Isherwood?"

Her slow, steady heartbeat and shallow breathing were his only response.

****

"Hallo, the house!" John called out from his position atop the coachman's seat. The carriage rolled to a stop on the pea gravel drive. The hour was late, but as he suspected, someone was up to receive them. Probably Moses. Light cascaded out of the windows and gave the cottage a cheery yellow halo.

He hopped down to the ground, a smile lighting his face at the realization that he didn't need to bother with clambering down the ten foot height. Without waiting for the coachman to make his way down, John opened the door and threw down the steps himself. As he expected, she was still completely knocked out. It was amazing what a small dose of laudanum could accomplish.

He scooped her up into his arms, refusing to pay attention to the womanly feel of her soft curves and focusing on his footwork instead. It wouldn't do to have her go flying when he stepped over the threshold with her in his arms.

The front door opened and Moses, silhouetted at the opening, stood holding a lamp high in the air.

"Good evening, Moses," John said as he entered the house.

Moses was struck dumb at the unexpected arrival of his master. John laid Miss Isherwood on the fainting couch which took up one wall of the front room. A fire crackled in the hearth. A book lay open on a small table next to which, a wingback chair stood.

"Educating yourself, Moses?"

"No, sir. You know I can't read. Most of my time has been spent upstairs, assisting Mr. Isherwood."

"Is he doing worse then?" John asked, leaving Miss Isherwood's side to speak quietly with the servant.

"Aye. The blood satisfies him, but I'm afraid, he's just ailing."

"Ailing." John rubbed a brow with one hand. It was disconcerting to note how much he had improved by ingesting human blood. Was it possible there was a correlation between the types of blood consumed? Were Mr. Isherwood's problems the result of an inability to process animal blood? In which case, if they were able to get Mr. Isherwood regularly supplied with human blood – and his daughter would be the donor who made the most sense if he was even capable of it – it was possible that he would make a full recovery.

John sent Moses upstairs to request that Mr. Isherwood join him. He needed to leave himself before the night grew much older. And he didn't want Mr. Isherwood to awake and discover his daughter appeared to have been turned.

Fifteen minutes later the gentleman joined him. He rushed over to Henrietta, concern and fear wrinkling his brow.

"I don't believe she has suffered any permanent damage." John said without preamble.

Mr. Isherwood inspected her with all the diligence one might expect of one who was a surgeon.

"She was drugged?"

"Yes. It was a temporary measure. I was afraid she would try to resist and she was so exhausted, I thought some enforced sleep might do her good."

"What's this?" Mr. Isherwood gasped, holding her wrist toward the light. His skin took on a greenish hue. "Dear heaven, please tell me daughter was not attacked."

"She was. But not in the manner that you fear. If I have your word that you will not tell anyone about what I am to tell you, I will tell you everything I can."

John recounted the whole story from beginning to end. Or most of it. He could not share the moment that he had with her when he melded into her memories. It was too precious a thing. Nor could he share in any great detail his meeting with Lord Wellesley.

More than once he was obliged to pause in order to give Mr. Isherwood the opportunity to take steadying breaths, or, with trembling hands, to brush back the wild curls that framed his daughter's sleeping face. She slept on, blissfully unaware that she was faintly snoring. Her father dabbed at the corner of her mouth with a handkerchief.

"As a father I must ask it, and thus I remain undisturbed that the very question might impugn your honor, but may I trust that nothing untoward happened while she spent this evening with you?" Mr. Isherwood bent a gaze upon him so intent, John was quite sure the man was attempting to see his soul. And that an invisible cravat was slowly strangling him.

"You have my word, sir. Nothing occurred that did not arise out of a necessity to act. The situation was an intimate one, but that was beyond our control. We did everything we could to preserve her modesty."

Mr. Isherwood nodded. "How soon do you think we will have to wait before we see signs that she has contracted the disease?"

"Two or three days at most. My only hope is that because my blood was deficient before I fed off her, that her defenses will be able to combat it rather than succumb to it."

Mr. Isherwood kissed her cheek and drew a light blanket over her.

"Thank you for waking me, Mr. Grissom. If you will excuse me for a moment, I am going to have Moses bring me a hot bottle for her feet."

John was on the verge of offering to do it himself, but an impulse to stay and have this last moment with Miss Isherwood prevented him. Mr. Isherwood left the room.

John vaguely felt as if he was skirting some sort of temptation, though he did not care to think on it too thoroughly. He studied her face for several seconds, his feet traveling closer without his intending it. With her pale, thin cheeks, and dark rings of exhaustion under her eyes, it was not hard to imagine that inside her chest, a disease was spreading itself, perhaps slowly, but in time, with greater rapidity until she would struggle to draw a single breath.

They had enjoyed a moment of real solidarity, a true friendship, in those hours in the dungeon. He would miss having that sort of companionship. They would have to resume the formal, more rigid working relationship they previously had.

He lifted her hand up and kissed the tips of her fingers before stepping toward the door.

****

John rolled onto his side and rubbed a hand down his face. He cracked an eyelid. Despite the thick curtains, the room was not entirely dark. The ormolu clock on the mantel read four in the afternoon. He yawned and rubbed eyes that felt as if the sandman had made free with a shovel and the beach. And then he realized he was starting to get hungry.

The pangs came on quickly, more violently than he was used to. He shook his head, attempting to clear away the sleep fogging his brain. When had he last fed? Was it Henrietta? But no, the butcher's blood. Which was thoroughly disgusting, if temporarily sating. But that feeding had only been some eight to ten hours ago. His eyes rested on the clock again. Why was he hungry again so soon?

****

Keeping to the deep shadows of the alley prevented him from full exposure to the sun. With hands gloved, the collar of his head to toe leather cape flipped up high to mid-cheek, and his hat pulled down as low as he could over his face, there was nothing more he could do. It staved off the worst of the effects of the sunlight, but nausea and the hunger that was beginning to grip him in earnest warned him that he needed to move quickly. The skirt of his leather coat swept the ground behind him as he paced, sending dried leaves and littered papers skittering. He moved swiftly, but refrained from moving so fast as to seem unnatural. His breathing began to come quick and fast. The infrequent passerby that didn't move out of his way brought a feral growl to his lips.

But finally he was there. The smell of blood, animal though it was and tainted with the musty beginnings of the stench of death, set his jaw tingling in anticipated satisfaction. He paused on the threshold, struggling to force himself into a calm demeanor.

"Good sir?! May I help you?" A young man wearing a leather apron covered in blood, paused on his way toward the door. John cleared his throat.

"Aye. Do you have any fresh beef or pork blood?"

The man nodded and ducked into another room. A vision, a temptation, wherein John saw himself follow the young man into the room and set upon him, filled his vision. He squinted his eyes shut against the pull and planted his feet to the floor, willing with everything in him not to move. Finally, he prayed for the grace to refuse. He prayed to St. Michael. To Our Lady. He pressed at his temples, focusing every scrap of his being away from the foul temptation and towards heaven.

"Sir? Are you well?"

John dropped his hands and lifted his head. The man stood with a bucket in one hand.

"Yes. I – I had a… it's nothing. How much?"

"Six pence. Do you have a jug?"

"No. Here's a sovereign for the blood and the bucket together," John dug out the coin from a pocket, along with an address he had prepared. "Also, you may drop blood off at this address every afternoon and evening. Just leave it outside the servant's entrance. I have the billing information on the paper."

The butcher traded the coin and paper hesitantly, as if he didn't think John could be serious, but when he saw that he was, he nodded his head in appreciation and headed back to the front of the shop.

John took the bucket outside. Twilight was finally setting in. It would be too much to attempt to make it all the way home before feeding if he continued at the same pace which he had arrived. Casting aside his doubts, he allowed himself to move with all the speed which his new vampiric abilities allowed. To others, he would seem a trick of the light, a blur they were unsure they saw. Within seconds he was stepping into the servant's entrance of his own residence and the door was closing behind him.

He brought the bucket into the black interior of the pantry and then shrugged off his coat and tossed his hat. Without bothering to find a cup or dish, he lifted the bucket and began gulping the blood down. But one could only drink so fast. He choked and sputtered, and then resumed. He would have to make sure that he had a more steady supply of blood. This kind of hunger could lead to a frenzy

201

swiftly. He had no idea if this would be permanent. But he should probably take notes on the change in his condition.

When it felt as if his stomach could hold no more, he dropped the bucket to the table. There was almost an inch's worth of blood in the bottom, but he couldn't manage it... yet. He momentarily wondered if it were possible that rules of gluttony would apply, but considering that it was in everyone's best interest that he remain sated, he couldn't think so. Despite the lack of connection, as there had been when he had fed off Henrietta, the satisfaction of feeling full was enough. He walked to and fro several minutes before wiping down his mouth with a cloth and donning the coat and hat again.

He left the bucket outside the servant's entrance door and headed toward the laboratory. Of course, he couldn't do any of the microbial research, but that wouldn't stop him from working on a weapon to use against Waite. The man had gone to ground. When he appeared again, John wanted to be ready for him.

****

John opened the door to the laboratory. He sensed Henrietta present somewhere in the nether regions of the house. What it was that gave her away, he didn't know. Or maybe it was merely that that was where she was supposed to be. But no, he didn't think so. Ever since he had, er, 'Charlied,'' her he felt more attuned to her presence. He couldn't imagine having the feeling with multiple people. He shivered with disgust as he hung up his coat and hat.

"Mr. Grissom? Is that you?" She called into the stair well.

He stepped into the hall and peered up at her. "Aye. I'm going to put on a pot of tea and then I will be up."

"But you can't –" she paused mid-word and shrugged before waving him off. Her head pulled out of sight.

A few minutes later John reached the top of the stairs. A dustbin sitting in the hall was full of glass shards, shattered wood, and wrecked equipment. He picked it up and in a blur deposited it downstairs in the kitchen. Within seconds he was returned with an empty one just as she opened the door and stepped out holding his microscope. One of his stained aprons covered a dark blue walking dress that had cuffs down to her sleeves.

"Oh!" she said, surprise on her face. "Good afternoon, Mr. Grissom. Thank you."

He set the dustbin down and smiled at her. It was a relief to see that the dark rings beneath her eyes were gone. Her heartbeat elevated as heat warmed her cheeks. She wasn't unaffected by his presence. He realized the size of his smile was entirely disproportionate to the occasion. "Good morning, Miss Isherwood."

She chuckled and handed him the microscope. "I don't know if you will be able to repair that. Perhaps it's just as well that you can't use it."

"Have you eaten anything today?"

"Yes. I had a big luncheon at the chop house down the block."

"You are looking... healthy."

"Yes, thank you. I had lots of sleep. You, as well, seem, er, recovered."

He nodded and an awkward pause fell between them.

"I'll have to set up a new laboratory downstairs somewhere until we can cover the glass on the roof. Although, there may not be much point. I may have to find a new research facility altogether."

Banging sounded from below stairs. Miss Isherwood latched onto his arm, her fingers like talons.

"What was that?" she whispered. Her eyes found his. He held a finger to his lips, plucked her fingers off his sleeve and began creeping his way downstairs.

CHAPTER 16

"John?" Gerhardt's voice floated up the stairwell. John breathed a sigh of relief and ran down the stairs. He arrived at the bottom faster than he anticipated, leaving Miss Isherwood to navigate the stairs alone. He glanced back, wondering if he should do the pretty and escort her down.

Gerhardt's eyebrows shot up at the sight of his sudden arrival.

"That was fast. Where were you?" he asked.

"On the landing. The laboratory was ransacked."

"I saw the study. Did they take anything?"

"No." John held up the portfolio and box.

"What's that?"

"Waite's serum and my notes on it."

"Perhaps we should feel fortunate they didn't torch the place," Miss Isherwood said from behind him. The three of them moved into the drawing room where John set down his items and closed the curtains more securely. Evening was almost upon them, but he didn't care to risk exposure.

"Vampires don't usually burn places down. They've no affinity for fire," Gerhardt said in answer to Miss Isherwood. John went around the room lighting candelabras.

"What's all this?" John asked, nudging a large leather bag on the floor. Gerhardt picked it up and opened the buckles on the bag.

"This, my new favorite vampire, is our dominos. And this," Gerhardt pulled out a length of green satin, "is your costume for the evening, Miss Isherwood."

Her fingers settled into the satin. "My costume? For what?"

"One of my trainees tracked down Waite's modiste. Waite will be attending Lady -----------'s masked ball this evening. Prinny is supposed to be there as well. I have acquired us invitations."

205

"But you informed the Crown, didn't you? Won't whoever you answer to make sure the house is surrounded with guards to prevent his entering?" she asked.

Gerhardt pulled out his and John's dominoes. "No. If a vampire wants to get in, he'll get in. Unless there are people there who can prevent it. There are terraces, servant and service entrances, balconies, windows. We can't post a guard on each entrance without attracting the suspicions of the populace. And since we want to actually capture Waite this time, we can't demand that Lady ----------- cancel the event."

Gerhardt tossed the domino and a set of evening clothes at John. "You have some rooms here, don't you? If you don't mind, I'll leave you here and take Miss Isherwood to her residence so she can change.   "

"No," John said, shaking his head.

Gerhardt turned to look at him. "What is this, no?"

"There is no reason for her to attend. It just puts her in danger."

"I can take care of myself, Mr. Grissom," Miss Isherwood said.

"Would you kindly give us a moment, Gerhardt?"

Gerhardt gave a nod and left the room.

"I know you can handle yourself against a thief intent on your purse," John resumed. "But there is nothing you would be able to do against a vampire and I'll not have you put at risk."

"You aren't putting me at risk. I am. And why not? I'm going to die soon anyway."

"Please, Miss Isherwood, for my sake." He reached out for her hand, but dropped his hand back to his side before he touched her. "Where would I be without my most valued and dedicated assistant?"

"You are doing it much too brown, Mr. Grissom. And I am afraid I insist upon it. If Gerhardt feels my attendance would work to our advantage, than I must agree with him.

Plus the fact, I've never before attended a masked ball in one of the houses of the ton. Would you deprive me of that joy?"

"It will hardly be a pleasurable diversion if you are focused on finding Waite."

"She won't be." They turned to find Gerhardt standing in the door. John stepped back from Miss Isherwood and ignored the knowing glance Gerhardt favored him. "She is merely to add to your allure for the evening. I don't know if we will be able to carry off the ruse, but we are going to leak to Lady ------------ that the man in the green domino is a nabob, newly arrived in Town. You will be his wife."

"Why do I need a wife? Why can't I merely be a nabob?"

"Unless you want every unattached young woman batting their eyelashes at you for a dance, you'll go along with it. It's not quite the thing to be sitting in each other's pockets, but at least that will keep you out of the nosy clutches of the curious and the thrill seeking. I assume you both *can* dance?"

"Yes," John replied.

"Well enough," Miss Isherwood said. "I never had a dancing master, but my exposure to my father's friends have given me some experience."

Gerhardt nodded. "It will have to do. I would avoid anything with steps you are unfamiliar with. I don't care to see the both of you falling over your feet. That hardly goes along with the persona of a stately nabob."

"And why do I need to be a nabob?" John asked. "Do I have to be anyone? What is Waite's story for the evening?"

"I don't know. But it has something do with Prinny. And Prinny loves shiny things. He lives for novelties, flattery, and wealth. Of which you shall have all three."

"And being that close to his majesty, John will have a better chance at ensuring his protection?" Miss Isherwood finished for him.

John sighed. He didn't like it. He wasn't a man about town. He was no fashionable fribble who knew what to say to a lord, much less a prince. "He'll see right through me."

"If he does, you're not half the man I think you are. Now," Gerhardt's eyes took him in from head to foot. "I am quite sure I have your measurements down to a pin. A hired valet will be arriving in a few moments. He's been provided heavily with payment to keep mum on all counts – and for the temporary nature of his work – so please allow him to aid you in dressing. You will be all the crack, as they say."

Miss Isherwood turned a critical eye on John as well. His face felt heated even though he knew it wasn't. Did she like what she saw?

"I look forward to seeing you in all your finery, Mr. Grissom."

"I shall look like a bedizened fool, all dressed up pretending to be a fantastic character. Heaven help us if he should ask me to tell any stories."

"A word of advice on that head," Gerhardt said. "I would not recommend it. I suggest instead that you pretend aloofness and secrecy, but assume that he knows whatever it is you are being secretive about. He won't gainsay you for fear of appearing to be in ignorance of what goes on in his own realm, and, despite his ignorance, he will vastly enjoy the attention such esoteric knowledge will give him."

"How do you know him so well?" John asked, holding out the cape in front of him. It was a black affair of shimmering satin embroidered around the hem with an intricate eastern design. Altogether too rich for a man of his simple taste. But certainly affordable by a nabob.

Gerhardt tossed another item in his direction and John caught it out of the air. It was a domino that provided his face with almost complete coverage. Suddenly, its pair sailed through the air and again John leapt and snatched it.

"What *are* you doing, Gerhardt?" John asked.

"Testing your abilities. You are still quick."

"Yes, but I'm not on human blood anymore, so I suppose it will fade soon."

He studied the domino more closely. The mouthpiece was cut out, but the sides of the mask came down to cover most of the wearer's cheeks. A green jewel sparkled on the corner of one its gaping eyes, but other than that one small gemstone, it was utterly devoid of color. Its pair was also white colored with a matching green gemstone.

"If you'll notice, the smaller mask, the bauta, is Miss Isherwood's; the domino, your own," Gerhardt said.

Miss Isherwood lifted the bauta from John's fingers and held it out in front of her. John fitted his mask over his face. She did likewise. Her eyes were almost invisible behind the mask, but for a glint of light now and again. The white washed out the color on her skin and left her lips appearing a deeper tint. It gave her an oddly menacing look.

"Go. I will meet you there," John said, turning to Gerhardt. "But I'll need an extra fifteen minutes in the lab though."

"For what?"

"I have something special for Waite."

****

"I'm going to have an orangery someday," Miss Isherwood announced.

John pulled his thoughts away from the pleasurable path they had wandered onto – enjoying the full effect of Miss Isherwood's completed ensemble.

"An orangery," he repeated with skepticism. He swept Miss Isherwood in another direction, dodging other swirling dancers as they made their way around the brightly lit ballroom. They had allowed themselves the luxury of a waltz after they learned the prince had not yet made his appearance. Now, with an eye toward the landing where the regent would be introduced, John, rested one hand on her back and held the other firmly in his grip, careful to leave the proscribed amount of space between them.

Her green eyes narrowed at him and then she looked away.

"You needn't sound like it's such a preposterous idea."

"No. Of course not."

"One can't grow oranges in England without an orangery. And I've heard such praise for the health benefits of the fruit. I thought..." her voice died away. Her glance darted about the room, uncertain.

"What?" John prodded, encouraging her with the slightest pressure on their clasped hands.

"I thought perhaps to try it as a remedy for my illness."

"It is a sound plan."

"Is it? You didn't seem to think so."

"If anything, I was just surprised. You must admit, the topic of orangeries is far removed from the topic of you learning how to waltz, which we had been discussing only moments before."

"I admit nothing. It seemed a logical transition."

He moved her away from a looming potted plant and glanced down to find her staring up at him, eyes challenging, mouth set mulishly.

"You obviously believe so. And I'm not about to argue with a woman's logic, ergo –" John said.

Miss Isherwood gasped.

"What is it? What's wrong?" John paused mid-stride and then began moving them away from the other dancers. "Did you see him? Is he here?"

"No. I just realized there's another myth broken. Look." She nodded in the direction of an enormous mirror that took up the upper part of the wall close to them. "I can see you perfectly."

"Of course. What were you thinking would be the case?" They spun away from the mirror and toward the opposite side of the room where the stairs loomed.

210

"I had heard the *Afflicted* couldn't be seen in mirrors. And since we didn't keep any mirrors outside of those in our bedchambers in my house, I've never had an opportunity to test the theory."

"Didn't anyone ever wonder how the Afflicted maintained themselves without having mirrors to survey themselves in?" John shook his head. "Not to mention, more than one member of the gentry has mirrors in their dining rooms and salons. That could prove awkward – or at least inconvenient to a, er, an Afflicted."

A flash of red on the stairs caught his eye. He watched as, at the top of the stairs, a group of ladies and gentlemen parted to either side of the grand stair case.

A plump and lavishly dressed man with a brocaded red sash stepped forward on to the landing. John circled Henrietta around the dancers and off the floor. Timing was crucial.

It took several minutes before the dancers and orchestra became aware of Prinny's presence, but then a hush fell on the assembly and every guest performed their bow or courtesy as the Prince Regent was announced.

If John appeared too eager to make His Majesty's acquaintance, His Majesty wouldn't expect him to be any different than what he was accustomed to in his fawning entourage. If John didn't make himself available, however, there was no guarantee he would be introduced at all.

Around him, masked gentry jockeyed for position in two hastily formed receiving lines. The music died, but the buzz of noise and hum of voices more than made up for its loss.

Excitement filled the room. Few had had the opportunity to see his majesty. Other than appearing at court, an occasion that in itself could require an entire years' salary for a country yeoman, one wasn't likely to meet the Regent.

John couldn't help but feel excited, no matter what satiric cartoons the broadsheets printed of the man. Prinny might be a bloated profligate, but he was England's most loved and revered bloated profligate and, to his own surprise, John discovered he very much wanted to meet such an enigma.

John worked them toward the front half of the receiving line, hoping to shoulder a way in. It didn't help that he had to maneuver his dratted ceremonial sword in such a way so as to prevent it whacking every person they passed. A hand grabbed his arm.

"This way." A subtle Prussian accent gave away the owner of the voice. Gerhardt tipped his head to the side, away from the crowd, his face hidden by a black mask similar to John's own. John made free to grasp Miss Isherwood's gloved hand. He didn't want to lose her in the crush of people straining their necks to see the Regent.

Gerhardt confidently led the way through the crowd to a position near the front. The prince had begun working his way down the line, a press of people, members of his entourage, following in his wake. Silence fell on their end of the expansive room as young lords, ladies, and matrons hung on his majesty's every word.

"He's going to drop his snuff box," Gerhardt whispered. John watched as the prince shook hands with a foreign dignitary, a polite smile on his full lips.

"How do you know?" John whispered. Gerhardt opened his hand. John's eyes widened. In the vampire hunter's hand was the most ornate snuff box John had ever laid eyes on. Inlaid with the mother of pearl, ebony, and gold, its ceramic surface held an exquisite depiction of the Queen's residence.

"You are going to drop *that*?" John asked in whispered disbelief.

"I am." Gerhardt shrugged. "Don't worry. I tested it several times already. It won't shatter. Make sure you pick it up."

The prince was only one person away now. John had his doubts about the plan. He turned back to voice them to Gerhardt, but the man had vanished into a crowd of masks.

The prince turned to approach them and John tossed the snuff box with a clatter of noise. The eyes of the entire assembly sought out the source. The snuff box skittered across the floor until it came to a stop two feet away from the Regent, rocking back and forth on its curved belly.

John stepped out of the line and picked it up. He gave his majesty as elegant a bow as he could muster what with the sword all but clanking on the floor, and then held the snuff box out to him.

"I believe you dropped your snuff box, your majesty."

The regent's eyes lit up at the sight of the box sitting in John's extended hand. He raised his quizzing glass for a closer look and then took the box from John. "So. We. Did. Your name, sir? Who do we have to thank for this rescue?"

"John Abbot, newly returned from East India. At your service."

"The ruse was prettily done. We must admit, you have caught our attention."

The regent's eyes played over his face for several seconds.

"You will be so kind as to walk with us, Mr. Abbot," the prince resumed.

John turned to Miss Isherwood.

"I hope I am not imposing in making the introduction of my wife? I could hardly leave her behind. Who knows what death threats I should endure in the near future for forgoing an introduction to the Prince Regent?"

A belly laugh breached his majesty's lips and taking this for a sign of approval, John stepped over to Miss Isherwood and drew her onto the floor. With his heightened senses, he could hear her racing heart. She glanced up at him and licked her lips in what he supposed must be a bout of nerves.

But then the sound of a voice at the rear of the ballroom, audible via his vampiric senses, a voice he had dreaded to hear all night, made his head snap up in alarm. He searched for its owner, but with the crush of people, he could discover nothing.

Where was Gerhardt? It was difficult trying to search a masked crowd for a particular face. Even harder to do so without drawing a great deal of attention to one's own inattentiveness.

"John?" Miss Isherwood asked pressing his fingers. She tilted her head in the Prince's direction. "I believe His Majesty is waiting...."

"Beg pardon, my liege. I became tied up in a hand of whist and didn't realize the hour. But here I am, as promised." The booming voice drowned out all the other noise around them.

Miss Isherwood turned in horror, but John had been forewarned. Waite's black domino covered almost all of his face, as John's did. But unlike his and Miss Isherwood's costume, Waite's intimidating frame was entirely costumed in scarlet satin and velvet. The elegant pitchfork cum walking stick he balanced in his hand left them without doubt as to which character he was aptly impersonating.

"Ah, Waite! We are pleased you could pull yourself away." The regent surveyed the newcomer's costume.

"Does it meet with your approval, your majesty?" Waite made an elegant leg.

The prince settled a thick, speculative finger against his plump chin and stepped back. He made a circuit around the lord and then paused.

"Your tailor? Weston's, we presume?" the prince asked.

John was tempted to roll his eyes at the posturing. Every satirist would make a May game of Prinny by tomorrow morning. The ballroom was hardly the place to be discussing wardrobe. Fortunately, it seemed that for once Waite agreed with John, since he pulled out his quizzing glass and stared down at the regent with a distasteful moue of annoyance.

"If you insist, your majesty, I would have no recourse but to answer. But any man must object to giving away his sartorial secrets. And," Waite leaned forward to whisper, "there are the ladies to consider."

Inexplicably, Prinny chortled, as if they shared a private joke. He turned in a circle, his eyebrows lifting and demanding general agreement with his good humor. His court of admirers laughed politely. John met Miss Isherwood's puzzled glance and he pasted on a smile, chuckled himself, and nodded his head. Offering pointless laughter was the smallest part of their subterfuge.

The regent's eyes rested on Miss Isherwood, and to John's annoyance and displeasure, genuine interest kindled there. John finished making the interrupted introductions and then steamed at the nostrils as the Prince allowed his full lips to linger over long on her hand. Beside him, looking smug – as smug as one beneath a domino could look – Waite was a silent, hovering shadow.

"Abbot is lately returned from India, Waite," the regent said, by way of an introduction. "We confess we have a curiosity to see the estimable country ourselves. Shall we do it?"

"Any region that is favored by your presence should count its blessings." Waite's fawning drawl was enraging. Or perhaps it was the obvious satisfaction Prinny took in the empty flattery.

"If I may, your majesty?" John said. The regent nodded at him. John found Waite's eyes as he spoke. "England ceases to be England without her monarch. Your subjects abroad may clamor for you, but England without your presence is utterly lost."

The regent's eyes danced back and forth from him to Waite and back again. Even he could sense the unspoken challenges that seemed to cloud the air between them. "Yes! Yes!" he said, confounding them all. "We shall have a pleasure cruise, sailing from London to Brighton."

The party continued its way toward the end of the line, the Prince all the while pressing hands and assuring invitations to guests who outdid each other in flattery. Miss Isherwood stopped to raise her brows and give a slight shake of her head. John couldn't but agree. With such flummery around him, it was no wonder the prince didn't recognize the vampire that stalked by his side.

"How are we going to get Waite away from the prince?" Miss Isherwood leaned into John.

"I don't know. Is it too much to hope that Gerhardt has an idea? I don't relish the thought of going mano a mano with Waite, even granting my new improved abilities. But we should do something soon. I don't know if Waite's plan is poison, kidnapping, turning him, or something as equally seditious, but his majesty's guards –" John's feet stilled.

A passing waiter carrying a tray of champagne glasses had walked by. A peculiar silence from him in a world of heartbeats caught John's attention as much as an alarum bell.

"Never mind," John said. "I know exactly what he is going to do. Come on."

John stepped forward toward the group making its way down the receiving line.

"Sir?" A liveried footman of intimidating proportions hailed him. John kept moving.

"Sir?" The footman trailed after him. "I'm afraid Lady ---------- demands your presence immediately." *I'll* bet *she does*, John thought. Who knew what Waite had told the hostess to pull him out of the room.

216

He tried to hurry, but without using his vampiric strength to simply force his way through the crush of curious onlookers, nothing was conducive to quick movement. If he could just get close enough to knock the man's arm....

His fingers were but inches from closing on the waiter's elbow when a meaty fist pulled his hand back and twisted it behind his back, crunching as much of the life out of his fingers as possible. The footman.

John shoved himself back. It forced his shoulder out of its socket with a sucking pop, but with no other recourse but to fight off the man, even if in the middle of a ball room, he would have to take the pain. At least he knew he would recover. And with any luck, it would buy them time. His left arm useless, he spared a glance behind to see Waite watching the waiter approach his majesty. Even his altercation with the footman had not created enough of a diversion to prevent the man's approach.

"Henrietta!" John roared. Several women screamed and swooned out of pre-emptive fear, and then silence settled on the ballroom. Miss Isherwood stood mouth agape, her fingers reaching out to him from across three feet deep worth of people. "The glasses. It's in the glasses."

She took a tentative step forward, seeking out what it was he was referring to. Her eyes darted from person to person standing near his majesty. Some fifteen feet away, the prince, too, had turned to discover the source of the commotion. The waiter paused, unsure whether he should continue.

Henrietta began to discreetly weave her way through the crowd. The footman who had recently had John's arm locked behind his back now punched at John's head. Screams of horror from the ladies ensued. Suddenly an arm was tightening around his throat. John growled and just barely prevented an instinctive unsheathing of his fangs. Instead he jabbed the elbow of his good arm into the body of his opponent with as much force as he could muster. The man fell away. Within seconds of being released, John's shoulder began to knit again. The ballroom was turning into an all-out brawl as gentlemen assumed the worst and began attempting to help the footman remove the errant guest. An unknown man clung to his back. Another launched a kick to his belly. None of this was going according to plan.

And then, as if he was more attuned to her voice, he heard a scream of fright that cut through all the other panicked female voices. A terrific crash and the sound of splintering glass resounded throughout the room. Action ceased. A wild howl of pain pierced the silence.

With a feeling akin to panic, John took advantage of the moment to throw the man off his back and push his way through the crowd. A circle of people stood around Henrietta who lay half on top of the footman on the ground. Shattered glass and champagne from the tipped tray lay on the marble floor nearby. An acrid smell filled the air, even while the marble began smoking from some sort of liquid etching into its surface. Nearby, the prince Regent stood leaning forward, his fat hands supporting him on his knees, breathing heavily.

"Your highness!" John said and rushed forward. What if the prince had been hurt? The regent looked up and then jumped away in fright.

"Arrest him! Our cravat! It was our latest creation," the prince cried out.

The measured sound of redcoats filing into the room took the attention of the guests. John helped Henrietta rise to her feet. Her hands trembled and her cheeks were pale. The man on the ground still twitched as if in horrible pain, clutching at his eyes. A whiff of garlic met John's nose and his eyes began to water. He backed away from the vampire.

"Garlic water?" John asked. An unknown gentleman in a black domino and cape stepped forward to whisper in the regent's ear.

"Yes. Gerhardt gave me a vial," Henrietta whispered back.

"Smart man. Did he give you anything else?"

"A silver stiletto."

"Good, hold onto it," he said. He watched warily, waiting for the soldiers to arrest him. Where was Gerhardt?

"A madman on the loose? The footman?" The prince turned to look at Henrietta, a new light in his eye. The gentleman continued to whisper at his ear. Prinny nodded once and minced forward to John and Henrietta. He held out a hand toward John. John took hold of the hand cautiously and shook. Only moments ago the prince was ready to have him arrested. What was he to make of all this?

The prince released him. "It would please us if you and your estimable wife would visit tomorrow afternoon."

"We would be so honoured, your majesty," Henrietta said. John all but groaned and rolled his eyes at the sweet innocent voice that tripped from her lips.

While Henrietta dropped into a curtsy so low John feared she would fall on the floor, John bowed deeply from the waist. A whisper of air against his cheek told him the prince had turned away. The crowd parted as the Prince made his way out of the ballroom, a contingent of guards and the unknown gentleman at his elbow.

Guests began milling about. They sent speculative glances his way and kept a healthy distance. No one approached him.

"One would think with a tongue as silver as yours is –" John began.

"What is that supposed to mean?"

"Don't you think you were coming it a bit strong with his majesty, the prince?"

Henrietta stiffened.

"I have to work with what little I have, Mr. Grissom. I know I am not of the caliber of these courtiers. But I'm not completely without some understanding of finer behavior."

John bit his tongue. He hadn't meant to offend her. But he had. Why did it bother him how she treated Prinny, anyway?

"Apologies, Miss Isherwood. I presumed too much."

She dropped her head.

"You did."

John nodded, and then realized the guests were still watching them closely. Especially a new pair of healthy-sized footmen who appeared to be procrastinating on approaching him.

"I believe we have worn out our welcome, my dear," John said, offering an arm. "Shall we call for the carriage?"

"What about Mr. Van Helsing?"

"I will find him. Allow me to install you somewhere out of the way of prying eyes. I'm afraid your gown has somewhat fallen into disrepair," he said, lifting an embroidered placard come loose from its stitching.

Head held high, he escorted her out of the ball room. Behind them, a buzz of conversation took over the room.

"Who do you suppose that was?" John asked, referring to the unknown gentleman accompanying the prince regent. There was something familiar about the man that just eluded John's memory.

"I assumed you have friends in high places," Miss Isherwood said.

"Not me." John suddenly realized who it must be. The Secretary of the Foreign Office, Lord Wellesley, was no stranger to social events, but he had not taken advantage of the moment to make himself known. John must assume he had his reasons. If Gerhardt's employer decided to bring Henrietta in, as he suspected they would, she would learn who he was soon enough.

"Sit here," John said, leading her to a seat in the cloak room. He studied her closely for signs of hysteria. But the only indicator of her former panic was a slightly elevated heart beat and the pallor of her cheeks. The color went

220

almost unchecked by the white domino. "Do you require some sort of refreshment to strengthen you? A glass of ratafia perhaps?"

"No." Henrietta shuddered and shook her head. "Thank you. I require only a few moments to sit and recollect myself."

"I'll be back soon."

He left. Somewhere on the grounds, the conspicuously absent Gerhardt was no doubt attempting to handle the missing Waite by himself. John imagined he would need help.

A search of the card room, library, study, and receiving rooms produced nothing. He didn't like the idea of searching the private quarters on the third and fourth floors, but without knowing how Waite planned on escaping, or whether Gerhardt would have caught up with him in time, he figured he should.

Fifteen minutes worth of listening at doors and dragging in deep breaths through his nose had offered no greater clue than the lingering presence of Gerhardt in one of the hallways that led to the third floor gallery overlooking the ballroom. John took a moment to study the guests down below. Even now, no one was yet dancing. The orchestra was heroically attempting to resurrect the lively mood by sawing on their instruments as if it were going to be the last time they would play, but the crowd remained unconvinced. They were too busy discussing the events of the evening.

John headed for a set of terrace doors off the library. Couples separated as he stepped outside. He ignored them and ran down the steps into a garden that opened onto a back lawn. The barest scrape of noise caught his attention. He raced toward the sound, his feet a blur.

As John took in the scene before him, he had to grant Gerhardt credit for being able to injure Waite on a moonless night such as this. With only the lamps from the house to shed light on this corner of the lawn, he had yet managed to cut Waite across the shoulder with one of his silver blades. But Gerhardt struggled to breathe against the arm that was compressed around his neck. Waite's bent head was sinking into Gerhardt's shoulder. The Prussian's heartbeat was growing sluggish.

John yelled and launched himself forward. He threw a right at Waite's head. The vampire broke his bite. A wolfish smile spread across his bloody lips and touched the bottom corners of his domino.

"John."

Gerhardt patted at his front with one hand, searching for a silver stake. But Waite tossed him aside carelessly. The vampire hunter flew fifteen feet and crumpled against a low wall. Waite pulled out a handkerchief and dabbed at the side of his mouth where Gerhardt's struggles had resulted in a mess.

"Do you really think you can stop me?"

John thought about his advantages. They were not many. Waite was long accustomed to his superior strength. He had a whole head and shoulders on him, along with a full stone in weight.

Waite began stalking him in a circle, his red fire-like eyes flickering in the dark and completing the picture of his dramatic demon costume. John figured he must look about the same, only perhaps more civilized. John reached for his belt.

"Are you going to pink me with your toy?" Waite laughed.

John clenched his jaw and bared his fangs, wondering if Waite would take the bait. The vampire lord rushed at him. Almost at the last, John pulled the slender rapier free to meet his charge.

Waite did not have enough time to slow down. But from his long-fanged smile, John had the feeling he wouldn't have anyway. Waite couldn't know that embedded in the center of the razor sharp sword, thin copper tubing ran along its center from the hilt to just short of the tip – and held a quantity of liquid mercury–silver alloy.

If the thin, brittle tip broke off inside a wound as John had every hope it would, the silver alloy would pour into Waite's body. But in order for that to happen Waite needed to come in close enough for a deep thrust. Now he was too quick, too close. By the time the sword was free of its scabbard, all he could do was slash at the lord's red velvet doublet and move away.

Waite beat his chest. The wound on his shoulder was black with blood that refused to run. Waite turned on him again, but John danced out of reach even while the tip of the rapier carved a gash across the earl's broad chest. Waite shook it off, which meant that the tip had not broken. John lunged forward and slashed again. Waite tried to block it and the thin blade tore his forearm open and left the red satin dangling.

Waite howled with rage. His fingers clutched at his arm where the skin attempted to knit together. His eyes blazed red.

"You are a traitor to your race!" Waite snarled. Faster than normal human sight, he came at John, but by the time he reached where John had been standing, John had moved aside.

With Waite caught by surprise, John flew forward out of the shadows, thrusting. The point bit deep into the vampire's chest and scraped against bone. John pushed it home and threw his weight against the hilt from the side, hoping against all hope that the tip would find bone and snap off.

Waite gripped the blade with both hands and bayed in pain, but also in triumph. It was evident he thought he was invincible, that he could now simply take the trapped rapier from him.

Then John heard it. It was but the faintest click of sound, but the feel of it seemed to reverberate up the whole length of the sword. Seconds later, Waite groaned and collapsed to his knees as the silver alloy leached into his blood stream. He struggled to throw John off, but John gave a great heave and knocked him over backward. The point broke through Waite's shoulder and buried itself in the ground.

"You would kill an unarmed man?" Waite's pale skin began to fill with dark colored streaks.

"You're wanted by His Majesty's government. Kill on sight. Didn't you know?"

Waite bared his fangs one last time in rage, but then, as if he realized his body was about to fail him, his eyes stopped seeing John – *or perhaps*, thought John, *they were looking inward*. The vampire croaked out a denial even as webs of black capillaries bloomed their way across his skin. His flesh began to dry and crinkle. He sagged to the ground, his body seeming to deflate.

John backed away, the back of his hand across his mouth, holding back the nausea that overcame him, despite all of his vampiric abilities that argued illness was impossible.

Waite's skin began to flake and then the muscles, now dried strips of sinew, disintegrated before John's eyes, until all that remained were bones. But then even those collapsed on themselves to the earth as so much dust, leaving John's sword waving gently back and forth above empty scarlet clothes laid out in the shape of a man dressed as a devil.

John stumbled down to sit on the ground, his elbows on his drawn up knees. Within seconds Waite had gone from walking and talking to… ash. Is that what would happen to him if something – if he…? It was too terrible to contemplate. It only confirmed to him what he already knew, that he could not dare to hope for anything – ever, with anyone.

"If that isn't a reflection on our mortality, I don't know what is."

John looked over. Gerhardt had dragged himself into a seated position against the wall.

"How long have you been conscious?" John asked.

"Long enough to see that I'm glad you're on our side."

John snorted. He leaned forward and rested his head on his folded arms. Being a good vampire was exhausting.

Footsteps sounded on the pavement behind them. He recognized her by the rhythm of her heart and the smell of her perfume. All the strain of the past few minutes seemed to evaporate in the consolation of her presence. The light from a dark lantern shot across the scene and then was shuttered.

"Is anyone inclined to inform me of what is going on? You tell me you are off to look for Mr. Van Helsing. I sit there waiting for a half hour, only to find you relaxing on the back lawn."

John looked over at her. She waved a finger at him in the dark.

"You aren't invisible, Mr. Grissom. I can see you with your glowing lit-coal eyes. Well?"

John fought back a smile. She was all but tapping her foot.

"Would you like to join us?" he asked. "The grass is superb."

FIN

Reviews improve authorship! Please consider leaving a review of this book on Amazon, Goodreads, and/or Smashwords. Your input is greatly appreciated!

Page Zaplendam loves to connect with her readers and fans. Drop by her facebook page or website, pagezaplendam.com to chat her up.

Want more from the world of John Grissom? The following excerpt is from Book 2 in The Unofficial Chronicles: The Hellhound of Derbyshire.

The Hellhound of Derbyshire

"Well, this isn't awkward at all," Miss Isherwood said from betwixt the two of them. John looked down at her, a picture of health and beauty in a spotted pale yellow muslin and a flower endowed straw bonnet. His gaze went across to Gerhardt who, frown lines etched deeply into his tanned face, sat on her other side.

Since the only available public conveyance at the local mews was a high curricle (normally built for two), they were squeezed into the seat in a decidedly uncomfortable fashion. "It's a beautiful morning, and we are quite cozy, if you ask me," Miss Isherwood continued.

Van Helsing growled out something indiscernible and shifted his shoulders in attempt to make more room. John wisely said nothing, knowing by the restless hitch in Van Helsing's breath that the Prussian would make his thoughts known soon enough.

Miss Isherwood, proving her skill at the ribbons, expertly guided their hired carriage out of the way of a dray and cart and they continued down the street in the direction of White Hall.

"If Mr. Grissom had not sent away the hackney coach that brought me," Van Helsing finally said, "we should be ensconced in the capacious confines of a brougham. But no, instead my bulk must needs be forced into this corner."

"Deepest apologies, Van Helsing," John said, forcing a note of false cheer into his voice, just to annoy the grouchy vampire hunter. "We can drop you at the nearest stables and you may rent a hack, if you like. Of course, that will make you unpardonably late for our appointment with Lord Wellesley – and we are skirting the time as it is – but it isn't as if you need burden yourself with us."

Van Helsing humphed. Miss Isherwood slapped the ribbons and clucked at the carriage horse. John leaned back his head and released a sigh of satisfaction, soaking up the sensation of sunlight on his face.

"You are happy, Mr. Grissom," Miss Isherwood observed.

"Aye. As you say, it is a beautiful morning."

"And we have so many things to be thankful for. You have all the fresh, human blood thoroughly out of your system."

From his corner, Van Helsing groaned. "More's the pity. He's as puny as any normal human."

"Mr. Van Helsing, I really must protest!" Miss Isherwood said in his defense. "He may not be exceptional, but he's no slouch with his fists or a foil."

Van Helsing snorted.

"There's no pleasing some people, Miss Isherwood," John said. "I would suggest you continue recounting everything we have to be grateful for. I thought it a worthwhile exercise myself."

"Well, now that you are on animal blood again, you may obviously enjoy the sunlight. I am happy for you, in that respect. And now that you are able to withstand sunlight, you may resume your experiments and find a cure for your affliction."

228

"And, by the grace of God, yours too."

Miss Isherwood stared straight ahead, a tight, humorless smile touching her lips. "Perhaps."

She pulled up the reigns outside the broad façade of the Downing Street apartments. A waiting boy took the reins and they crossed the deep, neatly swept walk that approached the entrance to number 15.

Within the cool, dim interior of the marbled foyer, a footman divested them of their hats and then led them to an adjacent sitting room where they were told they could wait. A clock on the wall ticked away the minutes while a restless Gerhardt strode the length of the room.

After fifteen minutes, John was inclined to think there had, perhaps, been some sort of mistake, but he was determined to trust that all was well since Van Helsing showed no inclination to be impatient. The man had had dealings with the Foreign Office before, perhaps this was the norm.

Finally a step in the hall and the modulated voice of Lord Wellesley called them in. Van Helsing led the way behind the footman and once again John found himself in the study of one of the most obscurely powerful men in England: Lord Richard Wellesley, Secretary of the Foreign Office, the brother to Lord Wellington.

"Ah, welcome, welcome." Lord Wellesley strode forward from behind his desk and reached out a hand to Miss Isherwood. "My dear, delighted to see you again."

He greeted each of them in turn and then waved them toward the chairs which sat before his desk.

"I imagine you are thoroughly recovered from your escapades with Lord Waite? No slow initiation there. Excepting Van Helsing here, you were dropped into the game and you must needs sink or swim."

John nodded his appreciation for Lord Wellesley's concern. "I am happy to say I am as restored to my former self as may be."

"Not to say 'fully restored,' eh?" Lord Wellesley asked grimly. "Ah, well, your defects have proved a boon to your country – for as much as you abhor them. And what of you, Miss Isherwood? Have the monkeys welcomed your return?"

"Yes, they have. Thank you."

"Good. Good." He rapped his fingers on the desk for several moments. John and Gerhardt exchanged looks. Was the Marquess having one of his notorious, awkwardly timed, blackouts?

"Forgive me, I beg you," Lord Wellesley said. "I see you are wondering what I have asked you here for. As of a few moments ago, I was undecided in what part, if any, the Foreign Office should play in the situation at hand. It's arguably the Home Office to which your division, Bow Street Odd Crimes, should answer, but – well, it would be rather unfortunate should Secretary Beckett not take the news of vampires et al so well.

"Be that as it may, I have determined to bring you in on a case in Derbyshire." He paused to rifle through portfolios on his desk and then slid one across to each of them.

"You'll notice, first, that your discretion, as always, must be absolute," Lord Wellesley continued. "I will admit this is along the lines of a personal favor, but I think you will find the case worth your time and effort."

John opened his portfolio. A handwritten letter was the first document.

"You each have facsimiles of the original letter I received several days ago from a family friend, Mr. Sebastian Drysdale. He requested my aid in discovering who, or what, is terrifying their countryside. The locals have determined a young Irish woman is the source and are settled on a witch hunt, of a sort. My friends are deeply concerned for her welfare and have thus reached out to me. To relieve any questions you have as to why your *special* talents are required instead of using Bow Street investigators, have a look at the second page of the letter where Drysdale details the specific circumstances which have begun raising concern."

All three of them obediently turned the page. John held his breath in anticipation as his eyes skimmed the words.

'I am not one to run scared of things unexplainable or out of the ordinary. When I see a slaughtered animal, a victim of a local feral predator, I feel no reason to board up my doors and windows in the evening. But the utter depravity and severity of these attacks has raised concerns in not only my own household, but also in the village and surrounding areas.

Whatever animal has decided to visit our society is unnaturally large. By the measure of its paw print, it must be something along the size of a bear.

Unlike other feral beasts, however, it does not eat its prey, but only hunts and kills it in a most bloody fashion – a fashion which leaves the prey torn limb from limb. It begs the question as to whether some returned Indiaman's exotic pet has escaped its leash, or if perhaps we have a mysterious, roving band of Gypsies that are periodically releasing their bear.

Our villagers daily become more incensed. To add to the furor, last week two young men who had been hunting on land lying adjacent to ours swear they saw a wolf-like creature walking on its hind legs as they returned home

231

late in the day. You may imagine what consternation that has caused.

The local magistrate, one Lord Lionel Winton, has been unable to discover the source, but is concerned, as are we, about how this situation will play out for the aforementioned Miss Lillian Byrne. The local gentry have not yet taken up the rallying cry of the villagers, but I, personally, would not put it past them to eventually concur with the thesis that she is somehow to blame. Her Irish heritage is largely held to be a black mark against her, and her father, unfortunately, has not made himself agreeable locally.

Naturally, all such accusations of her involvement in anything so menacing are patently absurd. I have no doubt that, should you be kind enough to send us your men, they could not find a more docile and innocent young woman.

"The odds are high that there is a natural explanation for all of this," John said. "Perhaps a glut in the game supply and a lack of larger predators has resulted in seemingly unexplainable and strange behavior from the local predator population. Of course, having a naturalist along, someone with a greater familiarity of animal habits, could prove advantageous."

"No doubt," Lord Wellesley agreed. "But I am not open to seeking out a naturalist who is unaware of all the various aspects of the detail he will be assigned to – including your own, er, affliction, as it were. Thus, until such time as a naturalist is added to Odd Crimes, you shall have to make do. I am sure between the three of you a reasonable explanation of the occurrences will be arrived at."

"As pertains to having an insufficient grasp of animal habits, I want to assure you, my lord, I feel no such inadequacies," Van Helsing said. "I have not survived as long as I have in my chosen vocation without paying heed to the smallest details of my surroundings, even the animal ones."

John kept his face as neutral as possible – a difficult task with Miss Isherwood smirking at him.

"Excellent," Lord Wellesley said. "You are all three invited as the house guests of Mr. and Mrs. Drysdale They have staying with them Mrs. Drysdale's younger sister, Miss Olivia Moore. You are invited to stay as long as the assignment requires and, upon my orders, to have any requests pertaining to the case fulfilled as needed. Do keep in mind that the budget of the Foreign Office is not unlimited and there is a war going on. I will give you until tomorrow afternoon to unanimously decide. Should you wish to take up the Drysdales' case, you need only send word and I will have an unobtrusive traveling carriage sent round to collect you. I imagine you will have questions, but most of them should be answered in the portfolio."

The three of them were ushered out several minutes later, files in hand. Van Helsing came to a stop next to the carriage.

"A Hindoostanee coffee house has just opened up on George Street," he said. "I've been wanting to see if their service is any good. I will pass up trying to squeeze myself in that carriage and make my own way home. Shall I meet you at the laboratory later this evening?"

John looked over at Miss Isherwood for agreement before nodding his head. "We will have much to discuss."

Van Helsing left them on foot, his leather duster tails flapping behind him, his face shadowed beneath the broad brimmed hat he was wont to wear.

John handed Miss Isherwood up and then took up the ribbons. As the curricle moved forward, despite the seriousness of their errand his heart was light. He realized it felt like their excursion had taken on the nature of a morning drive.

He frowned. His relationship with Miss Isherwood was a professional one and it needed to remain so. The temptation to allow such familiarity as one might find between a courting couple was not something either of them could afford.

"I take it you won't be taking up the Drysdales' case, Mr. Grissom?'

"What's that?" John asked, surprised out of his woolgathering.

"You had the most gruesome grimace spread across your features. It does not bode well for the proposed visit to Derbyshire."

"Oh. That. I am undecided. While I am intrigued by the various odd aspects of the case, I don't care to enmesh myself in something that the local magistrate could as easily manage on his own."

"If a young woman is truly in danger and we can help her, I can't imagine your work, our work, taking higher precedence."

He expected such sentiments from her. After all, despite her high degree of intelligence and administration abilities, she had a woman's heart with a woman's sensitivities.

And it wasn't as if she was wrong. But weighing all things in the balance, he would have to determine whether his time was better spent working on a cure or haring after a mystery in the Derbyshire countryside.

"I suggest we take some time to review the portfolio and regroup at the appointed time. Careful consideration is called for. Shall I drop you at your home?"

Miss Isherwood clutched the portfolio against her chest. "Yes, that would be good. I can pick up several books for father as well. I should send word to him not to expect me until later this evening."

"I will, of course, escort you out to the cottage. Notwithstanding your abilities with a lead-filled parasol, I would feel much relieved seeing you home myself."

She slanted a small smile of appreciation at him.

"Who will be providing supper this time?"

"I believe Van Helsing is due to purchase victuals. But you're risking something along the lines of stuffed cabbage or Toad-in-the-hole, if you care for that sort of thing."

"And I assume you will sup at the cottage later then?"

"Just so."

He pulled on the ribbons and the curricle came to a stop outside her door. It's yet shabby front was still in need of a paint job, now more than ever since Miss Isherwood had had the foresight to remove the plaque announcing her father's medical practice. With her father attempting to stave off failing health by living in John's cottage in the country, they had had to shut the business down. The worn door now sported a rectangle of deeper black where the plaque advertising his business once hung.

"One of these days," John said, handing Miss Isherwood down from the curricle, "I will rope Van Helsing into coming along on a Saturday and refreshing the paint on your door."

"That would be very kind of you, Mr. Grissom. But I hardly think it appropriate for an employer to so

235

concern himself with the needs of his employees." She turned at the top of the stairs leading to her door.

John laughed at her and shook his head in disbelief. But he wouldn't deny her claim. If she desired to pretend that their relationship lay more in the direction of employer and employee rather than in the direction of friends, he wouldn't oppose it.

"I will send a hackney round for you at seven then."

He left her and made his way to his own lonely house. Within a half hour he had the fire blazing in his study, a comforting cup of tea at his elbow, ready to warm his hands and perfume the air. Beside him on the table, a brace of candelabras were alight, and the portfolio's innards were laid out sequentially on his desk.

He would have more than enough time to determine whether or not their intervention would be worth his time away from his experiments. Gerhardt had, in all likelihood, already made his decision before they had set foot outside Secretary Wellesley's door. Not that the man had shared it with him.

John picked up the sheet of parchment which most intrigued him. It was an amateurish charcoal rendering of a creature, mannish almost in appearance, but for an extended, gaping maw full of sharp teeth, and clawed paws for hands and feet. Had the two young hunters, Drysdale's artistic witnesses, actually seen such a creature? Or were they perpetrating an elaborate hoax and placing a young woman in harm's way in the process?

Made in the USA
San Bernardino, CA
14 December 2016